Dear Ni

C000083103

THE
FORGOTTEN
CHILDREN

By Isabella Muir

Happy reading!

Best wishes

Isabella Muir x

Published in Great Britain
By Outset Publishing Ltd

First edition published November 2018

ISBN:1-872889-17-4
ISBN:978-1-872889-17-7

www.isabellamuir.com

Cover photo: by Mike Wilson on Unsplash
Cover design: by Christoffer Petersen

For all those who are still searching…

Author's note

I was inspired to write *The Forgotten Children* by true events, but the characters are purely fictional.

Foreword

I confess that I knew nothing about Britain's child migrant policy before I met Isabella Muir at Falmouth University. Sadly, I don't think I was alone. While I am in no position to comment on the policy, I do feel able to write about the time and care Isabella has taken to research the subject, resulting in this final published version of: *The Forgotten Children.*

Isabella started writing *The Forgotten Children* for her dissertation on the Master of Arts in Professional Writing course at Falmouth. It was during those early stages, when she was crafting and planning the story, that I learned about the child migrants sent from Britain to Australia and other colonies. Isabella chose an important and sensitive subject for her final project, while I chose to write an action thriller. Our books could not have been more different, and it was a welcome change of pace and style for me to read Isabella's early drafts, and to follow Emily's development as a character, and Isabella's as a writer.

During the interim years, since reading Isabella's first draft, several things have happened. Emily has developed into a strong character, together with the essential flaws that give her more depth and allow her to tell her story, and to shed light on the plight of child migrants then and now. Isabella has also developed into a strong writer with a clean and gripping style of writing to be envied, and an inspirational story that has benefitted from the time, care and even love she has given it over the years since that first draft.

Love is at the very heart of *The Forgotten Children,* love in all its forms, but central to the story is the love of a mother for her son. Isabella takes the reader on a captivating and important journey as we join the search for Emily's son, all the way to its dramatic conclusion.

The supporting cast of characters are equally intriguing, contributing each in their own way to the story, and ensuring that we, the reader, are given a glimpse into one of Britain's darkest hours. I have my favourites, but I won't spoil the story by revealing them here. I will, however, go as far to say that there is a certain cliff top, the description of which, and the scenes that occur there, make me long to visit that place, to breathe in the sea air and enjoy the countryside as Isabella has described it.

Isabella's inspiration for *The Forgotten Children* came from real-life events and at its heart is a tragic story. But variation is the key ingredient to Isabella's book, with characters and storylines that overlap to give the reader a sense of several of the crucial issues affecting family life in Britain from the 1960s through to the 1980s. There is much to reflect on and much to enjoy.

The Forgotten Children has been a part of my life for several years now, and I am excited that it can now be a part of yours too.

Christoffer Petersen, author of *Seven Graves, One Winter*
Denmark
November 2018

Chapter 1
Brighton
1987

Mark is a casualty of a war I've been having since December 1967. A war with more than one enemy and only one true ally, my beautiful Irish friend, Geraldine. In truth, if it were not for Geraldine, I would have spent most of the last twenty years unattached and free from the emotional demands that inevitably come from any relationship. But Geraldine, Gee to her friends, can't bear to see me single. So I ditch one bloke, only to be introduced to another. If it wasn't so sad it would be funny.

Mark is the latest. We've been together just short of two years. He's funny, uncomplicated and a great dancer. All attributes that score him ten out of ten in Gee's books, and leaves me wondering why she didn't go out with him herself.

I can't imagine a time when Mark and I would ever be as synchronised as Gee and Alan, who have been together so long they even finish each other's sentences. Nevertheless, life with Mark is easy enough. We party late at weekends and usually crawl out of bed at midday, nursing muzzy heads.

But since a visit to the doctor confirmed the reason I had lost my appetite, I've been trying to pluck up the courage to tell him our partying days are over. We will have to leave our little house, with its terraced garden higher than the roof and find a place with a flat patch of grass and a few leafy trees.

Now, as I lay in bed with Mark beside me, I close my eyes tightly and picture our new garden, with a seat under an apple tree where I could sit and watch our child play.

And that is the moment I recognise the betrayal. I'm dreaming of a new life while my first born is out there somewhere, maybe living, maybe dead.

The bleeding started earlier in the day and as I turn onto my side, it gets heavier. It's a suitable punishment for a crime I took part in, albeit unwillingly. I try not to move for a few moments, foolishly hoping I can stop this from happening.

Mark shifts beside me in bed. I peer at the luminescent numbers on the purple alarm clock that sits inches from my face. The numbers flick silently as a minute passes, then another. It is 3.30am precisely when I use one elbow to nudge him.

'I think I'm having a miscarriage,' I say, keeping any emotion from my voice.

I feel him swing his legs out of bed. He turns the bedside light on. I am scared to move and with my back to him I can't see his face, but I can sense him trying to move himself from a deep slumber to waking.

'You need to ring for an ambulance. I'm bleeding.'

He walks around the bed and kneels, then runs his hand over my forehead. As he pulls the sheets and blankets away from me, I hear him gasp. I look down to see the worst of it. The blood has pooled below me, seeping across the bedsheet, like ink on blotting paper.

'Oh God, Em. I didn't know. You didn't tell me.'

'It doesn't matter now, just get me to the hospital.'

St Stevens is a fifteen-minute drive away. Mark guides me onto the back seat of our car, throwing a blanket down for me to sit on.

'It'll be quicker,' he says.

My dressing gown clings to my legs and I have a mental picture of me, standing at the kitchen sink, trying to scrub the blood stains away. Stupid. Pointless.

That evening he visits me in hospital. His work jacket doesn't completely hide the crumpled shirt he will have grabbed from the ironing pile, creases around the collar and cuffs telling their own tale. He holds my hand and talks, while I listen. His topics are carefully chosen; the vagaries of the weather, the problems he's been having with the clutch on his car. He asks me about the hospital food and laughs when I screw up my nose and pull a face.

Finally, he asks me how I'm feeling. I turn towards one end of the ward where a single window looks out onto the car park.

'Are you in pain?' he says, running his hand over mine as though he is trying to wipe away all that has happened.

When I don't answer he tells me about a development at work.

'Did I tell you Em, one of the partners is planning on moving to Norfolk? He's asked me if I'd like to head up the surveying team. Apparently, there are loads of barn conversions just ripe for development. Norfolk, I ask you, it's all cabbages and farmland.'

Mark is a quantity surveyor, by trade and by nature. He'll assess each situation and weigh up the likely consequences, before confidently deciding on a chosen route. I don't. Neither weigh up, nor confidently decide.

'But then I got to thinking,' he continues. 'Maybe a move would be good for both of us. It's peaceful there, so it'd be good for your writing. We can go for walks. Think of all those farm tracks - Ralph would be in his element.'

His mention of Ralph starts a feeling of panic in the pit of my stomach. He watches my expression change.

'He's fine. He's with Philippa. You know how much she loves him. He'll be half a stone heavier by the time we get him home.'

He looks around the ward. A nurse is moving from bed to bed, changing the water jugs.

'When are you coming home, Em, have the doctors said?'

I shrug my shoulders and close my eyes.

'You're tired. I'll go, but I'll call in tomorrow, same time.'

I open my eyes and attempt a smile. He touches my shoulder, but I pull away and watch his shoulders drop. He runs his hand through his hair, flicking back his fringe.

'I'll trim your hair when I get home, if you like, or are you going for the rock star look?'

He shakes his head and turns and I watch him walk away from me. He pushes the ward door open with such force it swings back with a threatening thud. The nurse stops what she is doing and casts a sour look in his direction.

The hospital discharges me the next afternoon. Mark is at work, but there's a chance Gee will have skived off early. I remember her telling me that one of her friends was throwing a midsummer party and, knowing Gee, she will want at least four hours to get ready.

I take a taxi to thirty-six Cumberland Avenue; Gee's house share and the place that offered me sanctuary when I first arrived in Brighton.

'Lord, you're pale,' she says as she opens the door, taking my hand and pulling me down the hallway into the kitchen. 'Are you going down with something? Don't you dare give it to me or I'll miss the best party for ages. It's

Poppy's leaving do, will you come? Say you'll come, bring Mark too?'

We drink coffee and I tell her about the miscarriage, about Mark, about Norfolk. The words tumble out and she listens without interruption. She knows my past, she understands my present and appreciates the possibilities for my future.

'You're thinking of leaving, aren't you?' she says, gripping my hand. 'Wait a few days, give yourself time to think a bit more. Whatever you do, you know I'll support you.'

'I don't know how I feel.'

'You need to rest, walk Ralph, breathe some sea air. Give yourself time. Mark is solid, he cares about you.'

'I know.' I don't want to think about any of it.

'Don't you have an interview lined up?'

A few days ago my agent, Natalie, phoned to say *The Herald* is planning to run a competition, with a set of my books as a prize.

'They want a feature about you,' Natalie explained. 'The life behind the writer, that kind of thing.'

During the early days in Brighton I spent all my free time in Paradise Park, watching the children. The roundabout was a favourite; an old wooden thing, with its red paint long gone, leaving a flake or two as a clue to past days. As I sat, watching the children making themselves giddy, the first story came to me so fast I felt as dizzy as the little ones who were hanging on tightly. Polly with her golden hair in pigtails, pink gingham dress and short white socks, following Peter, a year or two older and full of bravado. It was when Peter first swung over the water on the rope ladder that his quiff fell into his eyes and I could see the possibilities opening up in front of me.

Geraldine persuaded me to send my first book off to agents and when Natalie Larkin replied, I had to read the letter three times before I could take it in. The process for the first book was tortuous. Editing, re-editing and bravely accepting Natalie's suggestions as she helped to turn my rough, ugly duckling draft into a swan that graced children's bookshelves countrywide. It wasn't just the writing that was transformed. The Emily who had arrived in Brighton years before had changed. The dreadful mistakes of my past couldn't be undone, but the grief and rawness had dulled a little. By the time I'd written the ninth book Peter and Polly were approaching their teens and their Scottie dog, Ralph, had traded long walks for hours curled up in front of the coal fire.

Until now I've been lucky, managing to keep my private life private.

'My readers are eight-year-old kids, Natalie, why would they want to know about me?'

'Emily, don't burst my bubble, this is brilliant publicity, you should be thrilled. Indulge me, Emily, just this once?'

'Thirty-six-year-old single woman, lives in sin in a £50,000 terraced house, with a daft dog called Ralph. I'll write it for them, it's easier.'

'Give a little, will you? Just talk about your likes, your hates, music, what makes you laugh, personal stuff.'

I know I will have to meet her halfway, it's part of the deal. But I'm good at pretending, after all, I'm a writer.

I refocus when I realise Gee is speaking to me. 'Tell Natalie you're not interested in doing the interview. You've just had a miscarriage for God's sake. You need to rest.'

She stands to face me and holds me gently by the shoulders. 'I'm worried about you, Em.'

'I will do the interview, but I'm not promising anything beyond that.'

'Don't make any rash decisions. Your hormones will be playing havoc with your emotions right now. Wait a while until things settle again.'

I don't need to reply. She knows me well enough to know my life will never settle, not until I've completed a search I've put off for twenty years.

'Well, I have no intention of going to any party tonight,' she says. 'Alan will just have to make my excuses.'

'But you'll be missed. Honestly, I'll be fine.'

'Fine or not, I'm going nowhere except to get you home. Come on, we can call in on Philippa and pick up Ralph on the way. The last thing you want is him jumping up and knocking you over.'

I didn't think I would smile today; but as she links her arm through mine and we head towards the hallway, some of the blackness lifts.

'It's a while since Ralph has jumped anywhere, he's getting old.'

'Aren't we all?' she says, pulling a jacket off the peg by the front door.

We meander through the alleyway back to number nineteen Filbert Road; the place Mark and I have called home for the last year or so.

Chapter 2
Brighton

For now all I want to do is lie on my bed and drift in and out of that dozy state that means I don't have to think. Ralph doesn't usually venture upstairs, mainly because the steep staircase proves tricky for his aging legs. But today I need him beside me so that I can dangle my hand down and stroke his ears.

Time passes and I must have dropped off into a deeper sleep, because I don't hear Mark opening the front door. I'm only aware of him when I feel his hand on my shoulder and hear his voice gently encouraging me to wake.

'I was sure they'd keep you in another night. I've bought your favourite flowers,' he says. I swing my legs over the side of the bed, disturbing Ralph, who jumps up and makes his way downstairs, stumbling a little as he goes.

'I thought Ralph didn't do stairs,' Mark says, perching on the edge of the bed. 'I'll put the kettle on, shall I?'

He follows Ralph down to the kitchen and I hear Mark open the back door to let him out into the garden.

I ease myself off the bed, my limbs stiff and aching. When I got back from hospital, I didn't bother to change my clothes, despite Gee's insistence I change into my pyjamas. But now I strip off, grab a tee-shirt and some jogging bottoms from the chest of drawers and go down to the kitchen.

'Are you hungry?' Mark asks, pushing a mug of tea towards me. 'You look really pale, what did the doctors say?'

'Nothing a few days of rest won't cure. I'll be fine.'

'Will you?'

'You mean, will we?' I can sense he is itching to ask me questions, but right now I don't have any answers. 'How was work?' I ask him, as he potters around the kitchen, putting bread in the toaster and pulling out cheese and pickles from the fridge.

For a while I listen while he tells me about his day, watch him as he butters his toast and munches his way through it. I imagine Mark as a father, holding our child's hand as he walks him to school, teaching him to ride his first bike, kick his first football. But, as the thoughts tumble around my mind, I realise it's not Mark I'm imagining at all.

'Em, are you listening?' His voice brings me back.

'Sorry, I was drifting. What did you say?'

He pushes his plate away and takes my hand. 'Why didn't you tell me about the baby?'

I can't do this now. I can't pick over the emotions I felt when I was pregnant, the memories it reignited of that first pregnancy twenty years ago, the one he knows nothing about. I can't explain to him the sense of loss, a loss I've lived with since I was sixteen, only to have it magnified now as my second child isn't given the chance to live for even one day.

'I'm sorry.'

'It's not your fault. We can try again, can't we?'

His face is full of hope that there will be another chance for him, for us.

'I'm going to lie down, I'm just so tired.'

I go back up to the bedroom and crawl under the blankets. I listen to him talking to Ralph. I can't pick out the words, it's a low mumble that in the end must send me to sleep.

Much later, I feel him get into bed beside me. I turn to look at the bedside clock. It's just gone midnight. He puts an arm out to curl around me. I pull away from him and ease out of bed and whisper that I'm going to get a drink. But I don't go downstairs, instead I pad across the landing to the spare bedroom, pull back the covers of the single bed and climb in.

By the time I emerge in the morning, Mark has left for work. He's put the flowers in a vase in the centre of the table, with a note propped up in front that says:

Table booked at Pedro's tonight, 8pm

I look at Ralph. who is waiting expectantly by the back door.

'He doesn't get it, does he?' I say, to my bemused companion. 'But there's no reason he would.'

We both need to deal with the fallout of a pregnancy that should never have been; the result of too many summer parties and free-flowing alcohol, making the risk of forgetting a pill or three highly likely.

I drift through the day. Gee rings twice to check up on me and I reassure her I'm fine, knowing she will understand I'm not.

When Mark gets home, later than usual, I'm lazing in the bath.

'Did you see my note?' he calls up to me.

I can't bring myself to shout a reply, so I wait until he presents himself at the bathroom door. 'You okay?' he says, leaning against the door frame.

'Not sure I'm up to going out.'

'It'll help to take your mind off things.'

Imagining the conversation I know Mark will want to have dulls any appetite I might have had. I wish I could curl up in bed and stay there.

'Problems at work?' I ask him, trying to keep my voice light.

'No, nothing like that. I had to pick something up on my way home. Shall I join you in there?' He points to the bath.

'I've been in here too long already. I'll leave the water for you if you like, as long as you don't mind smelling of lavender and roses.'

He laughs and starts to undress. We move around each other awkwardly as I get out of the bath and wrap myself in a towel and he steps into the warm water.

An hour or so later and we sit opposite each other at a corner table in *Pedro's Pizzeria*. The waitress brings over a carafe of wine and a jug of water and we order our food.

'You okay?' I ask, watching him playing with the salt and pepper pots, moving them around like pieces on a chessboard.

'There's something I want to say, but I'm not sure how.' He glances at the other diners. The restaurant is busy, the place has only been opened six months but it has already developed a good reputation.

'You did well to get a table.' I follow his gaze around the room.

He takes my hand and squeezes it, but I pull away from him.

'I'll pour the wine, shall I?' I say, spilling some of the *Rioja* on the tablecloth as I fill our glasses.

When he picks up his glass I notice his hand is shaking a little. I wait for him to speak, knowing I won't want to hear the words.

'Let's try for another baby, Em. I know this one wasn't planned, that we've never spoken about kids. But it'd be great. We'd be great.'

I sip my wine and avoid his gaze. I wonder if he can hear the thudding in my chest.

'There's something else,' he says, pulling out a small box from the inside pocket of his jacket and putting it down beside my glass. 'Let's get married. I love you, Em, you know that.'

The thudding that was in my chest moves up into my head until it is pounding. I push my chair away from the table and stand.

'I'm sorry, Mark, but I can't do this. It's not your fault, it's me. There are things you don't know…' My voice tails off as he looks at me with such hurt on his face. It's only when I notice some of the other diners looking in our direction that I realise I've raised my voice loud enough to carry across the restaurant.

'What things don't I know? Sit down, Em, we can talk about it. Maybe it's too soon, I should have waited.'

'I want to go home.'

He throws some money on the table to cover our drinks bill and follows me out into the car park. We drive home in silence and once indoors I let Ralph out into the garden, while I warm some milk in a saucepan.

Mark sits at the kitchen table, watching me.

'I'll kip in the spare room so I don't disturb you,' I say.

He shrugs, but doesn't say anything. It's as though someone has built a brick wall between us and now we have to find a way to live in the space we've been given. But apart, not together, not anymore.

Chapter 3
Brighton

The next morning I dress and prepare myself outside and in, looking at the mirror and rearranging my face to show nothing of the turmoil I feel. I haven't cancelled my interview with the journalist; she's due in ten minutes. Ralph and I were out walking early. By the time we got back home Mark had already left for work. This time there is no note on the kitchen table and the flowers have been consigned to the bin.

The journalist arrives, she is prompt. Her lipstick and carefully polished nails match her skirt, which is pink and vibrant. I wonder how much of her wages she's spent on her Diana haircut and whether she too is hoping to find her prince.

'Coffee?' I gesture to her to sit on one of the dining chairs, one of Mark's purchases that favours angular chrome fashion over comfort.

'Can I call you Emily? I'm Jocelyn, but, of course, you know that. I find being on first-name terms with my interviewees results in a more open response.'

I'm tempted to ask her which text book had given her that advice. Instead, I smile and ask, 'Is this your first interview?'

She is like a young racehorse at the starting gate, desperate to hear the gun. I guess she is hoping to impress her editor, perhaps seeing the chance to move from the features desk to something gritty. A picture forms in my mind of Jocelyn, in her pretty skirt and top, with her notebook in hand, standing in a pool of blood beside a murder victim. It seems my writer's imagination is as active as ever.

As if she can read my mind, she asks, 'When did you first start writing, Emily?

'When I was young, at school.'

'And where did you go to school? Were you born around here?'

I have fallen into the first trap and need to think on my feet.

'I'll apologise now if I don't give you a great interview today. I'm not feeling too good,' I tell her.

'I'm sorry to hear that. Several people at work have gone down with a tummy bug this week, there must be something doing the rounds.'

I smile. 'Brighton has certainly helped to inspire me. There's a vibrant arts community here. You'll know all about it, I expect.' If I could turn the conversation, I would be safe. 'Are you interested in writing yourself, Jocelyn, fiction I mean?' It would be no surprise to hear that she is another would-be author searching for a magic route to success.

'Oh, yes, I've started a novel. I'd value your opinion to be honest. It's not the same as journalism at all. Writing for the paper is straightforward, telling people the facts. But writing fiction, well you have to make it all up. It's hard.'

I relax a little, certain I've succeeded in distracting her, but the success is short-lived.

'But Emily, it's you I'm here to find out about. You've written nine children's books now, it is nine, isn't it? And yet your readers know very little about you. You've been hiding yourself behind a bushel – is that the phrase? Well, you know what I mean.'

I wish Gee was here with her empty chatter.

'Did you model Polly on yourself as a child?'

I smile again. What could I tell her? That Polly's fictional life with her brother, Peter, was as far removed from my childhood as it was possible to be. And maybe that was the point. Writing fiction has given me a chance to create a story world where nothing bad happens, or at least when it does, that the drama of a scraped knee from a tumble off a bike, or a broken window from an over-enthusiastic game of football is neatly resolved with a happy ending. I didn't have a brother, or a bike. What I had were rules to follow and expectations to meet.

Despite myself I am back in Hastings. Mum is making me parade around the front room. It's the day of my first Holy Communion and I am a child bride. My white dress was knee-length and I wore a short white veil. I still have the photo dad took. My small gloved hands held my Communion gift; a prayer book, with an inscription inside, in my dad's handwriting, '*For our little angel on this special day*'. My white, buckled shoes were bought just for that day. I wondered about it. Even aged eight, I thought it strange, when money was tight, that I was able to have a pair of shoes I would never wear again. Dad took a photo of me with a newly purchased Instamatic camera. Mum bought a shiny silver picture frame and the photo sat on the mantelpiece beside the clock.

I remember the Sundays leading up to that day, the rehearsals, the catechism, learning the prayers by heart. Mum continually telling me how important it was that I didn't make a mistake, how proud she would be. I can still smell the priest's hands as he held the wafer, cold and antiseptic, waiting for me to open my mouth for the Body of Christ. I held it carefully on my tongue, scared to swallow, wondering what it would be like to eat someone's body. I didn't dare look up, believing that to raise your eyes was unholy in some way. Then when I bumped into one of the girls walking towards me, I realised I'd let my mother down.

Only souls absolved of sin could receive communion and so the day before my first Holy Communion I attended my first confession. I sat in the confessional box and looked through the brown wire mesh at a shadowy figure and wondered what sins I should tell him about. I'd read my book for a bit longer at night than mum said I could. I'd poked my tongue out at one of the boys when he said I had funny hair. Were they sins? Was I wicked, like it said in the *Bible*? Right and wrong were all mixed up. I asked my mother again and again to explain it. But it seemed there were no answers to my questions. It was simply a matter of following the rules and doing His bidding.

On my sixteenth birthday I removed the photo of my angelic self from the shiny picture frame and added devil horns in black felt-tip pen and it felt good.

Jocelyn puts her coffee cup down and picks up her pencil.

'We haven't managed to get much down so far, Emily. It's the life behind the author our readers are interested in. What about your own reading habits, did you read a lot as a child? What sort of books do you read now?'

I'd just finished re-reading *The Thorn Birds,* having sat through the TV series; a story of a priest who falls in love and breaks all the rules. The hypocrisy it represented reignited a visceral hatred of so much I had been taught as a child. Maybe books weren't safe after all. 'Music, I love music. Sixties, seventies, Beatles, Bee Gees, Simon and Garfunkel.' I stand and walk over to our record collection and flick through the albums. I can see from

Jocelyn's glazed look I'm not giving her what she wants and I'm starting to run out of steam.

'Another coffee? Or tea?'

I wish the phone would ring. Even Mark returning early from work would be a bonus. Until now, throughout the whole interview, Ralph has been lying at my feet, motionless. He's still in recovery from our morning stroll around the park, but desperate situations call for desperate measures. I move my feet, nudging him into life.

'Ralph, meet Jocelyn. Jocelyn, Ralph.'

'Oh, Ralph - like Peter and Polly's Ralph, great. Which came first?'

The next ten minutes are comfortably filled with the tale of Ralph's arrival and his recent antics, both on and off the page.

I was in Paradise Park, drafting *Peter and Polly's Trip to the Forest* when Ralph first found me. I was sitting on my favourite bench, pencil poised, waiting for inspiration. The sun was distracting as it lit up my page for a few minutes, before being hidden by passing cotton wool clouds. There was a queue for the swings on this first day of the school holidays and a crowd of older children were playing football on the grass, using jumpers for goalposts. I had a vivid picture of mothers scrubbing grass stains.

I'd unwrapped a banana to keep my fingers busy while my mind caught up. In a mad moment I'd discarded my jeans for the day, choosing a newly purchased orange skirt, short and frivolous. I was willing the sun to be warm enough to keep my white legs from turning blue. It was his cold, wet nose pushing at the back of my leg that first alerted me.

'Hello you. Are you after my banana? I've no biscuits and no ball. Sorry.'

He came around to the front of the bench and sat looking expectantly at me. Clearly, I had to make the next move.

'Where's your mum and dad then?'

Until then I'd always thought it was only in films, or children's TV programmes, that dogs put their heads on one side. I'd never had a proper conversation with a dog before. I had a lot to learn. He was like a lop-eared rabbit, one ear permanently cocked, the other failing miserably. The black and white patches covered his body randomly and his collar held no clue as to his name or owner.

'Hm, where do you live then? Do you know your way home?'

After a while he laid down at my feet, with his head in a patch of sun and his body in the shade.

'I can see there are a few things you can teach me about relaxation.'

He didn't follow me home that day, but when I returned the next morning there he was, waiting at the bench.

'I've got digestives, will they do? Have you run away? I guess we have a lot in common.'

Mark and I had only just moved in together so when my new four-legged chum turned up, Mark made it clear that this particular third party would indeed be a crowd. He made me report him to the local PDSA, but when fourteen days later he hadn't been claimed, I registered my new four-legged friend with the local vet. Naming him was easy; my storybook Ralph had kept me company for years.

At last Jocelyn has her story. It's only when she stops asking questions that I realise how tense I've been. A wave of exhaustion hits me, but soon she will be gone and the black times before Brighton, they could remain mine. I'm not prepared for her final question.

'Writing a book must be a bit like giving birth, worrying for nine months, then the final pain and hey presto, a new life. And your agent is the midwife, so to speak?'

I stand and walk over to the window. I can't let her see my face. The walls are closing in on me. I steady myself and sense Ralph nudge up behind me. For a moment I think I'm going to be sick and then a surge of anger floods through me. A few days ago I had to say goodbye to a new life who had barely had the chance to form, and somewhere out there is my son; every day of his life, since the moment of his birth, has been lost to me. Twenty years of distraction are ripped away, like a cheap sticking plaster, with the wound still gaping wide open.

'I'm sorry, but I really need to take Ralph out now. I'm sure you understand.'

Chapter 4
Brighton

Mark shouts up to me as he leaves for work, 'I'm off now, Em. See you later.'

The conversations we have had since the evening at *Pedro's* have just led us around in circles. Right now there seems to be no middle ground and all the talking has helped me reach a decision.

I come downstairs dressed and ready for our morning walk and Ralph is waiting. Something in his demeanour today makes me think he knows my plan. This will be the last walk around Paradise Park. The last for a while, or perhaps the last ever.

The park has been a favourite haunt for me since I arrived in Brighton. It's just across the rise from the back of Gee's house - thirty-six Cumberland Avenue - with a footpath that winds past two duck ponds, a meandering stream, a children's playground and some weather-beaten picnic tables.

The showers throughout April and May have kept the grass lush and almost peppermint green. Azaleas are bursting with candy coloured blooms and I catch the scent of yellow roses as we walk past one of the many well-tended flower beds.

I sit for a while on one of the benches beside the footpath. Ralph settles at my feet, occasionally lifting his head as other dog walkers pass by.

I've always struggled with anaemia and being a vegetarian hasn't helped. The miscarriage meant I've lost a lot of blood and when I left hospital they warned me I'd be tired for a few weeks. So, sleep should come easily, but these last few nights it's been impossible. Every time I doze off the dream returns. The first time I had it was the night I moved in with Gee. Since then it's recurred every few months, hovering, waiting for me to close my eyes.

It always starts in the same way; I am out with mum in a clothes shop. I am small, maybe four or five, and the clothes rails tower above me in a threatening way. She has a tight grip of my hand, then suddenly she lets go. The clothes tangle around me and I can't see her. The more I fight to free myself, the more I become tangled. I try to call out, but my voice is muffled by scarves, sweaters, overcoats. After what seems like an age, I am free. I emerge into one of the shop aisles and see my mother walking away from me into the street. My feet won't move. I am transfixed. My mother has gone and I am left behind. I wake from it, sweating and struggling to breathe.

When I first had the dream it made no sense. I had chosen to free myself from the tangle of my childhood. I walked away from my parents and learned to live a different life, one without the suffocation of duty and rules. But as the dream recurs, I recognise the truth of it. The lost child in the shop is not me; it never was.

Ralph and I wind our way back along the path and return home. I pack my belongings into two battered suitcases and a holdall, the same ones I used when I left the security of Cumberland Avenue to move in with Mark. I look through our record collection and start to divide the LPs into piles, mine and his, before realising it was a pointless exercise as I won't have a record player. But the books have to come with me. I work my way through the bookshelves, loading my notebooks into boxes. Now that my children's series is complete these early jottings are worthless. I should bin the lot. Instead, I make a pathetic attempt at hiding them by creating a top layer of first editions, with my dad's dictionary tucked in beside them.

As I move from house to car Ralph shadows me, never more than a foot away, so that once or twice I nearly trip over him. Once everything is squashed onto the back seat of my VW and Ralph is on his favourite blanket on the passenger seat, I return to the house one last time.

I'm walking out on a man who has done nothing wrong, beyond being in my life at the wrong time. Perhaps there would never have been a right time for Mark and me. I promise myself I'll leave a longer note than the few scribbled words I wrote all those years ago when I left my childhood home. I'm a writer so I shouldn't have trouble with the note, but I start it five times before the right phrases land on the page.

Please forgive me, Mark, but I have to go. I just need time and space to find the part of me that has been missing for too long. Take some chances without me. You've nothing to lose, no responsibilities, you're as free as the birds that settle on your buildings. Norfolk may be flat, but I've heard the beaches are lovely.

I've no idea if he'll understand. Maybe one day I'll be able to explain.

As I load the last few bits into the car I realise I still have my door keys. Hanging onto them is my chance to come back. I know Mark would let me. But we'd be like our beloved LPs, moving into repeat, with the scratches still there to make our lives hiss and crackle. I take the keys from my bag and push them through the letterbox.

I've never been a planner. In all the years I've been writing fiction I've tried countless times to plot and prepare, to lay out my chapters and have a clear sense of direction, all without success. Instead my story worlds just seem to create themselves once I hold my pencil over each blank page of my notebook.

I try the same approach now. I open a page in my map book, close my eyes and point. When I open my eyes again I see that my finger has landed on an island, but one I can drive to. I imagine the Isle of Anglesey to be empty and peaceful; it's as good a place as any.

'All set then?' I look at Ralph for reassurance to find he's curled up with one eye open to monitor events.

I pull away from the house and turn left into Madeira Road, finding myself heading towards Cumberland Avenue. If I see Gee now and try to explain, I am certain she will do her best to stop me leaving.

She has been my sounding board for twenty years, since the day I first met her in a steamy café in Brighton. My beautiful Irish friend, with a zest for life, who has stopped me from wallowing in self-pity many times. She is the only person who has heard the whole sad story of my time before Brighton.

I told her a few months after I met her, one late night, or early morning. We'd just got back from a nightclub, via Fred's fish and chip bar. Our housemate, Maria, was working a night shift and her boyfriend, Simon, was sleeping. The Merrydown wine loosened my tongue, helped by Gee's expressionless face. I was used to judgement and criticism; having a good listener was a blessed relief. But by telling her I had to relive every moment of it. I turned away from her and stared out of the window into the black night.

There was no harm in Johnny and me. He was a couple of years older and most of the girls fancied him. He had a quiff and a wonky eye and there was always a sense he was winking at you. We'd lark about after school. I'd been to his house a few times and he to mine. We liked the same music, and sometimes he'd borrow his dad's guitar and play *House of the Rising Sun*, while I jigged around and sang. When we needed more time together my gift for story-telling came in handy.

'I'm meeting Helen, we're taking a picnic,' I'd tell mum, or 'Mary's going to help me with homework.' I knew she wouldn't check; she trusted me.

It only happened once. He was gentle, there was a bit of fumbling and a few giggles. I didn't think I was his first, but when I saw the look of surprise on his face, quickly replaced with complete satisfaction, I thought perhaps I was. It was almost the same look he took on when he'd lit a cigarette, but more intense somehow. I felt quite proud in a strange way, that it had happened and that he'd chosen me, but looking back maybe we chose each other.

A few weeks later I played truant. I left home at the usual time, walked to the bus stop, but when the school bus came around the corner of Marley Lane, I turned in the opposite direction and kept walking until I reached the station. I bought a single ticket to London and got on the train, exhilarated and terrified in equal measure. Two hours later the train pulled into Charing Cross station. It was a grey February day and only the second time I'd ever been to London. I felt light and unattached. I could walk, get the Underground, buy a hot dog, anything could happen - I could make anything happen.

I walked the Embankment, alongside the Thames, amid the shove of commuters, shoppers, tourists. The grey sludge of water lapping at the river's edge was uninviting. River boats offered lunches and river trips and people queued, wrapped in scarves and hats, mittened hands holding steaming hot chocolate. I passed the first telephone box without stopping, but by the time I reached the second I was ready. It must have sounded like a threat, but it was never intended that way.

'I'm in London, on the Embankment, just walking and looking at the river.'

There was fear in the silence at the other end.

'Your dad will come on the next train; he'll bring you home,' was all she said.

Two days after my runaway trip to London I took the bus to Eastbourne and visited a doctor. One who wouldn't know me or anyone around me. The doctor confirmed what I'd already guessed, although I was never sure if the sickness came from the fear, or the other way around.

I spent several evenings standing in front of my dressing-table mirror, looking straight ahead, deciding how I would tell my parents. But all I could do was stare at the mirror in silence. There were no words to describe the terror that grabbed me during the long nights when I tossed and turned. Or the thoughts I'd had of throwing myself down the stairs. I'd sinned and sinners have to be cast out.

In the end I waited until dad had left for work. Mum was ironing. 'I'm sorry,' I said. I was sorry too - for them, for me and for the little seed inside me. But sorry wasn't enough. It never would have been.

Perhaps when you make one mistake it is inevitable you will make more. I shouldn't have told my mother when dad was at work. She had time to put her slant on it, point out that I'd committed a sin for which I should never be forgiven.

I told Gee how I'd been to the library, found a book that described it all. The biological reality that enabled a human being to emerge from a hole no bigger than the top of a milk bottle. My baby and I were of the same flesh and yet separated by it. I sang to him, talked to him, dreamed of the days we would never have. His first steps, his first words. My love for him grew as did my hatred for my mother.

During the last few weeks of my pregnancy I became a recluse, my life getting smaller as my child grew within me. I ran out of clothes that would fit me. My mother even suggested I wear my dad's jumpers in the end. She told me to stay indoors, to make sure no-one saw me in my state of disgrace. I would sit for hours in my bedroom watching the clock hands moving slowly around as I felt him wriggle. Then after nine long months, I waited for ten days beyond my due date. Nine months of apprehension, followed by ten days of fear.

When the pains finally started she rubbed my back. It was early morning and dad hadn't left for work so she told him to go up to the phone box and ring for a taxi. As far as I know it was the only time my mother ever went in a taxi. She was silent in that taxi while I screamed. Hours later my baby emerged, ripping my body and my heart. Stitches for one, but not the other. The book had told me of the miracle, the joy of holding your own creation, said it would wash away the physical.

I never held him, not even once. 'It'll make it harder for you,' my mother said.

'Harder than what,' I screamed at her, 'nothing can be harder than giving up your child.'

Another mother would hold him, see the pout of his tiny lips as he sought sustenance. My breasts would ache for the want of him, leaking wasted goodness until, like me, they were damned.

'You're just a child yourself,' mum said. 'You'll have another, you'll be married and things will happen in the right order, the way God intended.' I can see now that she made me hide behind her fears.

The night after I gave birth I dreamt I was walking the hospital corridors and there was a woman asleep with two babies beside the bed; she had stolen my child, my chance of motherhood. In the dream I grabbed him back, held him close, and jumped on a bus to our new life. Me sitting on the back seat of a double-decker bus, with my hospital gown wrapped tightly around the two of us.

But in the morning I woke from the dream, hot and wet, from the running, from the milk flowing, to be instantly chilled by the empty space beside me.

When I finished telling Gee everything, I put my head on her lap and wept. She hugged me and said nothing. I knew she understood and that was enough. It was a long time before we spoke of it again.

I drive past Cumberland Avenue. It's time to move on.

Chapter 5
Anglesey

The congested city roads widen out to congested motorways, then queues of cars on dual carriageways, each heading for a specific destination. I have no planned arrival time. Only tiredness will prevent me from driving all night, all day.

I switch on the car radio, then quickly switch it off again. Music can be soothing, but not voices, not hourly news reports of gloom and doom, wars, crime, political ramblings. Without music the drumming of the traffic passing has a comforting rhythm to it. I glance over at cars as they overtake; a wife or girlfriend pointing at a map, shaking her head at the driver's comment, disagreements that no longer have a place in my life. An old Ford Estate sidles up beside me and as it passes, a child sticks his tongue out at me, proud to be escaping reprimand while his parents focus on the road ahead.

The traffic slows; there are roadworks. For a while I come to a stop, giving me a chance to scan through the cassette tapes that are scattered across the passenger seat. I grab one and shove it into the cassette player, smiling when I hear the whining sounds of one of Beethoven's violin concerto. Mark might have rock star hair and a love of disco dancing, but his classical record collection still takes pride of place beside the record player.

A car horn sounds, bringing me back; the traffic is moving again. An hour later and I'm clear of the worst of it; muddy verges replace the hard shoulder, rain water runs in rivulets beside the road, sometimes pooling and splashing up against the car. I need the windscreen wipers on full speed to combat the spray from each passing lorry.

A brightly painted sign for a café lures me off the road into a car park, before I realise mine is the only car. The parking bays are filled with lorries; it's as though I've stepped into a fairy tale, where I am tiny in a land of giants.

Opening the car door I breathe in the smell of frying bacon; five years of vegetarianism and I'm still tempted. A young man, tattooed arms showing below his sodden tee-shirt, walks in just ahead of me, holding the door open and smiling.

'Morning. Nice day for driving,' he says.

Avoiding his gaze I notice that all the drivers raise their heads from their steaming plates, briefly checking this customer who doesn't quite fit with the grease, the cigarette smoke, the *Pirelli* calendar beside the till displaying barely dressed models advertising tyres. Perhaps I should turn around and drive on.

'Come in, luv. Don't mind these boys, they're just pleased to see a pretty face for a change. It's mostly ugly mugs in here.'

The waitress wipes a table with a cloth, scattering crumbs to the floor.

'What'll you have then? How about a cuppa to start?'

I nod and notice the other diners are now refocused on their food and newspapers.

I sip my tea and picture Mark getting home, finding the note. I'm certain he will miss Ralph as much as he misses me. He never fooled me with his pretence of not liking Ralph. I would listen as he sang or chatted to him when he thought I was out of earshot. He would make up ridiculous poems and recite them to Ralph, who would look quizzical, as though he was expected to know the last line.

'Are you alright there?' the waitress puts her hand on my shoulder. 'You've gone a bit pale. You look like you've had a bit of a shock.'

'It's been a long drive,' I say, as if that's enough to make her understand.

Once I'm back in my car I sit for a while outside the café, gazing at the phone box. I should ring Mark, to make sure he's alright, to try to make him understand. It won't be easy because I'm not even sure I understand myself.

I get out of the car and walk slowly towards the phone box. Once inside, I sift through the change in my purse, placing the coins neatly in a row, ready to drop them in, one after the other, as though that simple sequence will make the conversation easier.

I dial the number and wait. The phone rings the other end, on and on. I curse myself for not buying an ansaphone. Mark wanted one, I didn't. I only have myself to blame - for all of it. He's not at home, or he's choosing not to answer. Either way, there's no more I can do.

I drive on until I spot a petrol station up ahead and pull in. I walk around the car and unlock the petrol cap; but before I take the nozzle from the petrol pump a young girl approaches me.

'Can I help you? It's not self-service, you see.'

'Sorry, I didn't know. Yes, thanks, can you fill her up for me?'

I find my gaze transfixed on this young girl's midriff. She is pregnant, maybe six or seven months.

'You're staring. It's a bit rude to be honest, anyone would think you'd never seen someone pregnant.' Her voice brings me back.

'Sorry, it's just that…'

'I know people think maybe I shouldn't work here, what with the fumes and that. Not good for the baby. But needs must. It's a job and money's important when you've got a little one on the way. You'll know what I mean. You got kids? Grown up now, I expect.'

I take out my purse.

'That'll be £8 please.'

I give her a £10 note. 'Keep the change,' I say, wondering whether she is insulted or grateful. 'Good luck with it all, the baby I mean.'

'Thanks,' she says and moves on to the next customer who has pulled up behind me.

As I continue my journey the road widens, I drive through a tunnel that takes me through the heart of a hill, going from light to dark and into light again. Then there's a bridge and suddenly I'm on an island. The terrain is rugged hills on one side and the sea dropping away on the other. The road signs are in two languages, I am entering a new world and I can't go much further west without falling into the sea.

I pull into a driveway shaded by the elm trees that give the place its name, *Four Elms Guest House*. I walk up the path, through a pristine front garden bursting with colour co-ordinated flower borders, neatly planted pots and hanging baskets. I take in the scent of the creamy white roses that wind their way up the wicker screen beside the front door. I ring the bell and wait just a few seconds; a young woman opens the door, her hands are floury and a smear of flour on her nose makes me smile.

'Well now, you've caught me. Monday's my baking day. Come on in. Are you after a room? Would you prefer ground floor? We have one that opens out onto the back garden, which might suit Master here?'

'Yes, thank you. He's well behaved, he rarely barks.'

'Just not on the bed or the furniture. Barking we don't mind, as long as it's not after lights out.' She smiles and I realise she's teasing me. She goes to a jar on the hallway desk and takes out a biscuit, holding her hand out flat in front of Ralph who doesn't disgrace me and gently removes the biscuit in a well-mannered fashion.

'I'm Catherine by the way, and what's your name?' she asks him, in a tone that suggests she expects him to answer.

'Ralph,' I say, 'his name is Ralph'.

She shows me to the only guest room on the ground floor.

'We're quiet at this time of year, but we do have a family arriving later, hence the baking. They're having a birthday celebration. I thought I would do something special, a cake with candles and all. What do you think? Oh, listen to me, I'm rambling. William is busy planting out the back. Ralph might like to explore once you're settled.'

There is nothing co-ordinated about the bedroom furnishings, which makes it all the more cosy. The patterned woollen throw is burgundy, the curtains primrose yellow with spidery trails of ivy winding up towards the pelmet. The bedspread is cream and there are coloured rag rugs scattered generously over the pine floorboards.

I put my holdall onto one of the wooden chairs, and look out of the French doors to see William kneeling beside one of the flower beds, patiently turning over the soil with a small trowel. He has a large straw hat perched precariously on his head and he's wearing a checked shirt. He reminds me of one of the characters out of the Wizard of Oz.

I open the French doors and let Ralph out to explore the garden, while keeping half an eye on him. He is intrigued by the chickens, which are well protected in a fenced-off area at the bottom of the garden. William is chatting to Ralph as I approach.

'Morning. I've explained to your young man here that chickens are not for eating or barking at and he seems to get my drift.'

'I'm sure the treats you've been giving him helped him to remember his social etiquette.'

I have stumbled on a little piece of heaven and I want to stay here forever.

That night I sleep like I haven't slept in months. As I wake, I stretch my hand down beside the bed to stroke Ralph's head and caress his ears.

I think about Mark. Our early morning moments together were often the best of the day. I would drift between waking and slumber and he would linger a few minutes to wrap his arms around me. I would recount a dream, or we would both be silent, listening for Ralph's padded footsteps as he moved to the bottom of the stairs, ready for our arrival.

Gee introduced me to Mark, despite my insistence that I was content with the single life. It was only six weeks since I'd finally talked my way out of a brief relationship with a lad called John, whose only real passion was speedway. Too many late nights, stood around a freezing track convinced me that this relationship was not for me.

But Gee was certain that Mark would be just right. 'Emily, meet Mark. Mark is the only person I know who dances better than Michael Jackson. Mark, Emily is my best friend and a famous children's author. She is also man-less at present and badly in need of a fella.'

'In your opinion,' I glared at Geraldine, as I held out my hand to Mark. 'I apologise for my friend, she rarely knows what she's talking about. Let's see that dancing then.'

We spent the evening on the dance floor and the early hours walking along the seafront. He liked to talk and I've always preferred to listen and even though his jokes were obvious, they made me laugh. He was coming to the end of his surveyor's training when we met and lived in a pokey one-bedroom flat over Maurice's chip shop. We dated for six months, by which time my toothbrush was a permanent fixture beside his, in the only bathroom I've known that permanently smelt of fish.

But then his landlord decided to increase the rent and we knew it was time to move on. For a couple of weeks I spent my days in estate agents and my evenings walking around the local area, looking at *For rent* boards. There was little in our price bracket and what there was needed to be pulled down and built again. I'd narrowed the list down to a choice of one and booked a viewing.

'I'll list the reasons why we should say no and then you can decide,' Mark told me when the agents first showed us the place. 'The garden's higher than the roof, it overlooks a power station and there's damp in the kitchen.'

'You're in the trade, Mark, what's a bit of damp to a man of your abilities and maybe we'll get a discount on our bills, the electricity won't have as far to travel.'

The terraced garden of number nineteen, Filbert Road, rose up from the back yard and I could see myself sitting in a deckchair looking at the night sky.

'I'll be closer to God and perhaps He'll do me some favours for a change.'

'Well the paintwork's got to go, perhaps you can do the stripping?'

We shared a secret smile as the estate agent pretended he hadn't heard.

We found the deposit and the landlord was happy for us to spend our evenings and weekends replacing the yellowing gloss with Briwaxed banisters and doors. As each room was finished we celebrated by putting on a favourite Dire Straits track and dancing around like teenagers. Mark and me, me and Mark – it would be fine; although in truth I knew it never could be.

A few days have passed since I pulled into the drive of *Four Elms* and Ralph and I have settled into a comfortable routine. The beach walks are wild and invigorating and Ralph has remembered how much he likes the sea. On occasions we explore a walk across the headland, where I can look out over the windswept coastline. On the other side of the wide bay is a rising slope, part covered with thick woodland, framed with hedging, creating a patchwork of greens and browns.

I know I need to start planning my search for my son, but for now the thought of driving on is senseless. I return from our afternoon walk and ask Catherine if we can stay another week. She smiles and pats the seat beside her.

'If you're planning on staying longer, Martha Jones has a cottage to rent, it'll be cheaper in the long run. I have her number here if you're interested.'

The comfort of Catherine and William's hospitality, her freshly baked bread and his freshly collected eggs and home-grown tomatoes are hard to walk away from. But having my own space to relax into will help me decide on my next step. After a phone call to Martha Jones I decide to take her up on her suggestion. 'Go and take a look my dear. See if it'll suit you first and then we can agree a price and whatnot.'

Following her directions I find *Martha's Cottage* just half an hour's walk from the guest house and as I approach it I'm confronted by a bland, pebble-dashed wall, with a small window, made to look smaller still by the wooden crossbars that fill the frame. I can see a door, but I can't see a way to reach it, the garden is fenced all around with wire netting. I scan its perimeter for a gate. I wonder about a place that keeps people out, or perhaps in. Ralph tugs at his lead and pulls me around the edge of the wire fence and it's only then I realise I have approached the cottage from the back. A wide path of crazy paving leads up to a front door. The door looks as old as the cottage, with an iron latch appearing to serve as its only lock. A rusty bell hangs from a rope beside the door.

I meet Martha at the cottage the next day and we agree terms.

'Can I take it for a month...for now, at least?'

'Oh yes, a month, is it? That's fine with me. You've got my number if you have any problems. Electric's a bit temperamental, but Colin down the road, at *Winter's Wild*, he'll help you out. His number's there, pinned on the board. And if it's a plumbing problem, well now Jimmy is the best plumber on the island, he should have retired by now but folk just won't let him.'

This community appears to be as safe as the one I created in my storybook adventures. Peter and Polly's tales have brought me success as an author, but for the last few months I've stopped writing and now I'm in Anglesey I've got too much time to think. Maybe thinking is what I've come here to do, but on a whim I decide to place an advert in the local corner shop.

'Private tuition: English - all levels. £8 an hour.
If you are interested, telephone Anglesey 245643 or contact Emily at Martha's Cottage.'

I buy an ansaphone and eagerly check it each day, but I'm not surprised when I receive no messages.

Chapter 6
Anglesey

I stand to eat my breakfast because sitting at a table feels too much like permanence. Ralph is delighted as crumbs fall from the kitchen counter. He hoovers them up and circles my feet, keen not to miss these unexpected offerings.

It's the first morning in my new cottage. I've spoken to no-one since leaving the open-all-hours shop at 6'o'clock yesterday evening, laden with groceries and a few household essentials. I've sought solitude, only to discover how lonely it is.

After breakfast, Ralph and I walk up to the shop again and the bespectacled shop assistant welcomes me, 'Hello again, you're a new face, just moved in is it? Or are you on your holidays?'

'Just passing through,' I say. 'It's very pretty'.

She isn't fazed by my reticence; there's no questioning as she packs my shopping into bags, purchases that belie a customer who is 'passing through'.

'Oh, well, pretty, yes I suppose you're right. Me, I was born around the corner and after a lifetime in a place you don't see it, do you?'

I genuinely don't know. I haven't had a lifetime – not in Hastings or in Brighton. And yet I can see them both still, their beauty and their ugliness. I listen to her chatter and wonder how I will explain to this kind Welsh lady why I keep returning to her shop day after day, week after week.

'Still passing through?' she will ask me.

On our walks Thomas is always there in my mind, hovering like an early morning mist that refuses to clear.

But today I'm thinking of his father, Johnny. I've imagined Johnny many times over the years. Sometimes he's a musician, the lead vocal in his own band. Not rock, not pop, but something in-between. Our shared love of music was one of the things that brought us together.

Some afternoons after school Johnny would go home, pick up his dad's guitar, then meet me at the recreation ground. There were plenty of quiet spots to sit, under the trees, away from the play park. He'd strum a few chords and then start singing, a huskiness to his voice that wasn't there when he spoke. I'd tease him and tell him he sounded like Elvis. He knew Elvis was my least favourite singer, so he'd dig me in the ribs and try to sing deeper, putting on a different accent. We'd be rolling around laughing, the guitar laid to one side and music forgotten.

I often wonder what made him choose me. He could have had his pick of the girls. His wonky eye gave him a permanent cheeky look, like he was always smiling. The girls would hang around him, pretend to like what he liked. But not me, I thought he was out of my league. I'd been playing netball one day and I saw him, standing on the sidelines of the court. I wasn't even any good at netball, which made it all the more embarrassing having an audience. Then, when the game was over, he came up to me and asked me out. Just like that. I remember blushing and feeling pretty stupid about it. I was almost looking over my shoulder to see if I'd been mistaken, if he was talking to someone else, not me.

Our first date was hanging out in a café, *DiMarco's* it was called. We found a table in the corner, under the stairs. We had mugs of tea and laughed that our parents wouldn't believe it. We were never into alcohol, even though some of our friends used to sneak bottles out

39

from under their parents' noses. But Johnny and I would stick to tea and sometimes we'd stretch to jam doughnuts.

Simple times, simple pleasures, far removed from the sinful act that brought my mother's punishment down upon me.

A while after I told my mother I was pregnant, Johnny and his family moved away from Hastings. They were renting their house, so it was easy, no selling or buying involved. They didn't have much by way of possessions, but hundreds of books. I remember the books, lined up in order of height, with no thought for subject or category. I wasn't there the day they left. Mum had made sure of it. A pact, perhaps with Mrs Selmon. Johnny wasn't to know mum said. One family destroyed was enough. But when he told me they were moving I hugged him tight and said goodbye. He promised to write, I didn't expect him to and I was right.

When I think of Johnny now, I see him hand in hand with a beautiful wife, some children, two or three perhaps and his ebony quiff, edged with a trace of silver.

We've been exploring the beaches, but today we take the same walk around the headland that Ralph and I took from *Four Elms*. It's a bit more of a stretch from the cottage, but worth it. This area of beach is popular with windsurfers. In the late afternoon on windy days vans of all shapes and sizes pull up into the car park that runs beside the beach. We look down on an assortment of young lads rushing to don their wetsuits. It's exhilarating to watch them as they take their boards and sails and push on into the waves.

Looking out from the edge of the cliff it's possible to imagine the wind blasting away regrets and sorrows. We walk across the headland and I spot someone moving in

40

the distance but by the time we reach the spot they have gone. The next day I retrace our steps and Ralph runs ahead of me barking. As I catch up with him I see someone sitting on a bench. The man is wearing a thick duffel coat, with a flat cap pulled down around his ears. Ralph runs over to him and starts to bark and as I get close, I see the stranger has a dark beard and weathered skin. He bends down and strokes Ralph, but a minute later the man has gone. I call Ralph and we walk in the other direction.

When we return to the headland walk for a third day Ralph is ahead of me again. He runs straight to the bench, sniffing and searching for his new friend. But the bench remains empty for the next few days.

I keep an eye out for the stranger as I stroll around the village. It's such a small community it seems inevitable I will see him somewhere, walking, waiting for a bus, or queuing expectantly like the rest of us, for the first crusty rolls from *Bryony's Bakery,* where fresh Welsh cakes beckon from the window each time I walk past.

Many of the local faces are already familiar, although I don't yet know their names. I've named these nameless folk and imagined a life for each of them.

There's Mrs Cherry, named for her red nose that peeps out from the bundle of woollen scarf and hat she wraps tightly around her. She trots past my cottage on the way to the shops (how soon I have claimed ownership). On her return her gait is slow and measured, as she balances herself with evenly laden bags. Carrots, potatoes and onions in one - ready for the soup she makes daily for her family, who are all able to come home for lunch. No sandwich at a desk for them. The other shopping bag contains all that is needed for a home-made steak and kidney pie. Mrs Cherry has no need for the convenience foods that the supermarket offers, she believes the way to protect her family is to feed them well.

I frequently cross paths with Mr Ironside. He is returning from his daily walk to the paper shop, with the *Times* tucked under his arm. His Trilby hat and grey overcoat, the uniform of a commuter. But this commuter has chosen to stay put in his home town. I have chosen law as his profession. I see him advising and guiding the townsfolk as he peers over pince-nez spectacles, nodding encouragingly as he listens to their plans for a house purchase, or a change to a will. His caseload is straightforward, no litigation, no divorce, no acrimony. This is a community in harmony.

I've named them all. Miss Smart, the primary school teacher with hair pulled back into a tight ponytail. On weekday mornings she jogs past my door at 6am in yellow and black Lycra and matching running shoes, regardless of the weather. Then at 8am she walks past, with her bag of books and sensible shoes, ready to enthuse her class of eager minds.

I am entertained by this cast of characters. Miss Smart, Mr Ironside and Mrs Cherry and the rest of them would all make wonderful characters in a story I know I will never write.

But among them all there is no sign of the stranger on the headland.

Then today we return to our cliff-top walk and Ralph runs off towards some bushes, barking.

'Ralph, come, this is no time to be chasing rabbits.'

Ralph emerges from a clump of gorse but he is not alone. The stranger walks beside him.

'Hello, sorry about my dog, he's always on the lookout for food and probably thinks he has more chance with someone else than with me,' I say, as I sit on the bench that is helpfully placed to get the greatest view of the seascape below.

'Good morning,' he says and sits down at the far edge of the bench. I'm grateful for the space between us, but sense that perhaps he needs it more than I do. I can't place his accent, but I know it's not Welsh.

'Ralph seems to have taken a fancy to this bench. I hope you don't mind. It gives him a good view of potential squirrel territory. At least I think that's what it's all about.' I'm not sure why I'm apologising for sitting on a public bench.

'He has a good eye for special places. I like the view too. It's uncluttered.'

He pats Ralph, but keeps his head down. I have yet to see his face.

'I'm Emily and this is Ralph.' I don't know what else to say and I find myself blushing.

He nods, but says nothing and a comfortable silence hangs between us. For a while the three of us look out at the view. The stranger strokes Ralph and I notice his hands are weathered, but clean. His trousers are shabby and patched and his shoes are tied with string. I wonder what has brought him here and why he has chosen this place.

I stand and clip Ralph's lead onto his collar, sensing he will be reluctant to go home.

'Goodbye then, perhaps we'll see you again,' I say as we leave.

'Yes,' is all he says. I'm encouraged by it, although I have no idea why.

When we get back to the cottage I find a note. It has been pushed through the letterbox, but hasn't dropped to the floor, it's still there caught by the brass flap. I pull it out to see an envelope with no stamp. Hand-delivered. I open the envelope and read the short note:

Dear Miss

I saw your advert offering English tuition. My son is nine years old and is struggling a bit with his spelling and whatnot. Could I book a lesson for him with you? Maybe one hour a week? My address is 7 Primrose Avenue.

Many thanks
Mrs Davies.

This is good, walking is fine but it's not just my legs that need stretching. For now it's just one lesson but there's a chance it could lead to more. I write a reply and walk down to Primrose Avenue, which is just five minutes from *Martha's Cottage*.

Chapter 7
Anglesey

These days in *Martha's Cottage* are my first experience of living alone. I moved from life at home with mum and dad, which was safe and ordered, to a life with Gee and her house-mates, which was anything but. Then, when I moved in with Mark I thought I would learn what it was like to be a grown-up, to be in a partnership where we were equals, but the scales were constantly shifting. The only time I felt in control was when I was putting pen to paper. Dad's dictionary is still with me and I look at it now, reflecting on how this lexicon of words has coloured my life.

It was Dad's dictionary that led me to one particular morning at primary school, when I was just ten years old. Sister Mary Cynthia and the other angels of the church were a constant and comforting presence in my life, gentle and forgiving. She took the boys for football; all five foot nothing of rotund nun, her habit comfortably snug around her like a second skin. Her referee's whistle hung from a cord around her neck. The shrill, sharp sound would warn the lads who liked to push the boundaries that she would stand no nonsense. She was firm, but fair and always ready to laugh.

I couldn't have been more than six or seven when I asked her how old she was.

'No more than a hundred,' she'd say, with a twinkle in her eye. Thinking back she might have been in her forties, maybe not much older than I am now. There was a surety in her that I never saw in the other female figure in my life, my mother.

The day when Sister Mary Cynthia beckoned me up to the front of the class, all eyes were focused on the purple

45

tin that was sitting on her desk. Congratulations, or similar, floated above my head as I gazed at the unmistakable colours of my favourite chocolate bar, emblazoned on the lid of the tin.

'Don't open it until you get home, Emily,' she instructed. Two long hours before I could run into the kitchen and announce, 'I won, I won,' to my mystified mother who probably didn't even know I'd competed.

It was a short story competition and I don't even remember what the story was about, but I recall the thrill of having won that coveted tin of chocolate bars. All for me. I took the tin to my bedroom, opened it and carefully took out each treat, laying my winnings on my bedspread, arranging and rearranging them in the order I planned to eat them.

Mum and dad never asked to see the contents of my treasured tin and I never shared a single bite with them.

A few days after receiving the note from Mrs Davies, the child and his mother are at the front door of the cottage. I open the door to see a pale-faced child, holding tightly to his mother's hand.

'Hello,' she says, 'this is Billy and I'm Gwen.'

'Hello, come on in. Billy, would you like to sit here?' I indicate a chair beside the table I have cleared, ready for our lesson. Gwen hovers. I sense she is anxious.

'Um, shall I stay?' she asks.

'It's really up to you. Perhaps we should let Billy decide. Are you happy for your mum to leave us to our studies and maybe come back in an hour?'

He looks from her to me and then down at Ralph, who has been sitting quietly beside the table, waiting for someone to notice him.

'Can I pat your dog?' he asks.

'Of course. Let me introduce you. Billy, this is Ralph. Ralph, Billy.'

Billy kneels down beside Ralph and ruffles the fur on his head, rubbing his ears and sending Ralph into wriggles of delight.

'Billy's always wanted a dog. But I told him, maybe when he's older. They're a big responsibility, aren't they?' Gwen directs her comments more at Billy than me.

Billy is happy for Gwen to leave him to spend an hour with Ralph and I'm hopeful that somewhere there will also be time for some tuition. I'm pleased the lesson plan I've prepared is all about animals, which will hopefully distract Billy from worrying about his difficulty with words. As we work through the lesson I can see that Billy is a bright lad. Gwen has explained how he struggles with his English, having missed a whole term of school the year before. He caught a cold that turned into pneumonia. For a long time he wasn't well enough to go outside and then when he was, his energy levels stopped him from doing a whole day at school.

'It was easier to keep him at home,' Gwen explained, looking at the ground as though she's embarrassed. 'I didn't think about his schooling, not really. I wanted to keep him safe. I've only got Billy you see. His father died when Billy was six. An accident at work.'

'It must be a struggle for you.'

'It's just the two of us, so it hasn't been easy. My parents died in a car accident before Billy was born and his other grandparents emigrated.'

I wonder how it would have been for my child growing up without a father. Throughout my pregnancy my mother had told me how impossible it would be for me to care for a child when I was barely a child myself.

But brave people overcome huge challenges and now I know I would have been brave enough.

Gwen tells me she is a school dinner lady, a job she was lucky to get, which gives her the chance to see Billy off to school and be home in time to have his tea ready on the table.

'There are things we have to do without, but at least we've got each other,' she says. I wonder if money is the real reason a dog is out of the question. When Gwen returns at the end of the lesson, I say, 'If Billy wants to come walking with Ralph and me some time he would be very welcome,' adding, 'Ralph would like that too.'

'Can I mum, can I really?' Ralph senses the excitement and starts to run around in circles.

'Look mum, Ralph's dancing.'

Martha's Cottage is the perfect size for Ralph and me, with two small bedrooms nestling in the eaves, the angles of the ceiling timbers creating patterns of light and dark. I enjoy lying on the bed with the curtains partly open to watch the changing shadows as the sun sets and the moon rises.

The cottage is full of history and memories. The chairs are assorted, nothing matching. The centrepiece of the living room is an old Welsh dresser, its shelves lined with plates chosen for display. One depicts a Westie playing with a ball in a lush garden, another a snowy Christmas scene with robins perched on a log. The quilted bed cover has delicate hand stitching and I wonder if Martha made it, or if it's a treasured family heirloom. The cottage breathes happy family gatherings, Christmas, birthdays, cosy winter Sundays and long summer days.

I've slept late this morning, after several sleepless nights when my mind won't settle. I come to and listen to Ralph's patient pacing at the bottom of the stairs. I put on my slippers, wrap a cardigan over my nightie and go downstairs. Ralph is so pleased to see me at this late hour he does a twirl, dancing in approval.

'You're a joy, do you know that?' I say to him, expecting a response. He wags his tail and looks hopefully at the bowl of apples. His early morning treat is a carefully quartered apple. He knows just how many pieces are available, should I dare to sneak one of them.

'Okay, you win, I'll get dressed and we'll go for a wander.'

It's been raining on and off for the last few days. I put my boots on and grab Ralph's lead. Just before leaving I take a pencil and an empty notebook from the sideboard drawer.

Ralph knows where we're headed, but is in no rush. He stops at every tree or bush along the way, as interesting smells divert his attention and I'm reminded how much of nature's wonders I've missed all the time I spent rushing around Brighton. I am completely absorbed in this train of thought, looking around me, intrigued by the tangle of bramble and gorse that sits in clumps across the cliff-top, that I don't see the gentle stranger walking towards us. Ralph pulls on the lead and it's only then that I look across the footpath. The man's rucksack is slung over one shoulder and his duffel coat is unbuttoned. I can see his lips pursed as if he is whistling, although he is still too far away for me to hear, as the wind blows the sound away from me. But Ralph's ears and nose are alert, he hears the whistle, and detects the scent of this interesting new friend. It's enough for him to tug frantically on the lead and his tail starts its circles of ecstasy. The stranger has seen us and lifts his hand to wave. I wave in reply, then drop my hand as quickly as I raised it. Ralph and I walk towards the bench as a couple are just leaving. They walk away arm in arm along the footpath. Ralph is distracted with the scent of rabbits and I sit, grateful my long raincoat provides some protection from the damp seat. I take out my notebook and pencil and start to doodle, childish attempts at daisy chains and trees in full leaf appear on the page.

'Hello,' his voice takes me by surprise. Ralph stops sniffing and appears at the stranger's feet, tail wagging and eyes shining.

'Sorry, I was deep in thought.'

'Don't apologise,' he says, as he sits beside me and glances over at my book. 'Not an artist then?' he says, smiling.

It's the first time I've really seen his face. I notice a deep scar running down his left cheek.

'No. And no hope of ever becoming one either,' I say. 'Good job it's stopped raining.' I'm annoyed at myself, reverting to inane discussions about the weather.

'I had a dog once. A long time ago.'

I can hear sadness in his voice. I try to imagine life without Ralph and realise I can't, or at least I don't want to.

It's started to rain again. A gentle drizzle I don't notice at first, until I lift my hands from my knees and see the dry patches underneath.

'There's a calm about this place, despite the turbulent weather. I can see why people have lived here their whole life,' I say, hoping he doesn't think I'm prying.

'I'm a visitor here, just like you. I was looking for peace and I found it here.'

'Did it take you long? To find this place?'

He smiles, the weathered creases around his eyes softening his gaze. I guess the outdoor life has added years to his appearance, but I snatch a closer look at his face and realise he is younger than me by several years.

'Towns and cities are not for me,' he says.

'Do you live nearby?'

He nods his head towards a stretch of fields to the right of us. 'That's home for now. For as long as they have work for me. And you and Ralph?'

'I'm just having an extended holiday, trying to recharge.'

'It's none of my business, but I'm guessing there's more to it than that.'

I look away from him, bending down to stroke Ralph who is sitting beside me, waiting for his next adventure.

'Don't hesitate too long,' he says. 'You'll only find peace once you start your journey.'

I've been in Anglesey a while and I'm missing Gee. I dial the number, hoping she'll answer. Instead, I hear Roger's voice.

'Emily? Good to hear from you - how are you? *Where* are you come to that?' My mind is racing, things have obviously moved on considerably since I last spoke to Gee. At that point Alan was still firmly in place and now it seems he's been replaced by Roger Black.

'She's not in', Roger continues. 'She's gone to a hen night, one of the girls from Black's is getting married next week. You might remember her, Melanie with the curly auburn hair and freckles. I'm on beans on toast, while your best mate is probably eying up the stripogram.'

Miss Smart is outside the phone box, hopping from one foot to the other. There's been a real chill to the wind all day and there's no shelter on this corner of the road.

'What shall I tell her?' Roger says, 'she'll want to know where you are. She'll be mad at me for not asking enough questions.'

'Tell her I'm fine and I'll ring tomorrow. Must go, someone's waiting for the phone.' The school teacher smiles at me as I leave the relative warmth of the phone box to face the blustery wind. We exchange a few words, then I pull my collar up around my ears and jog home. Home. I suppose it is for now.

Chapter 8
Anglesey

I don't ring Gee the next day. I need a plan before I speak to her. If the roles were reversed and she was the one needing a plan, she would have crossed all the items off the list by now, but I haven't even made one yet.

That's the task I've set myself for today; but when I come to write the list there are only questions.

Where is my son?
How do I find him?
Will he want to be found?
Why did I let him go?
Why has it taken me so long to look for him?

As the list of questions grows I realise the enormity of the task. Finding Thomas after twenty years is one thing, but dealing with the fallout, the explanations, the recriminations, is another.

This time when I ring Gee she answers.

'My wandering friend. God, I've missed you. Where the devil are you and when are you coming home?'

I can picture her sitting on the bottom stair, cradling the phone with her head on one side. I was always telling her she'd get a pain in the neck from doing that and her inevitable reply was that she had one already.

'You're a dark horse, going out with the boss. What happened with Alan?'

'It's a long story, but in brief we decided we needed space from each other. And then within two weeks my space was kind of filled again. It turns out Roger was just waiting for me to be available to make his move. He reckons he's always fancied me, since my first interview.

I've told him I don't believe a word and it's up to him to persuade me, which is the fun part. But enough about me, what about you?'

She tells me Mark has been calling round every day, hoping for news about where I am, when, or if, I plan to return.

'How is he?'

'How do you think? Getting thinner by the day and desperate for answers.'

'You haven't told him anything?'

'It's not up to me. But he didn't deserve what you did, leaving like that with just a note, no real explanation. It wasn't exactly your finest moment.'

There have only been a handful of times when I've been angry with Gee. The last time was when she accused me of hiding from reality. I'd replied with some scathing remark about her doing the same most nights by polishing off as many vodkas as she could afford. The row had escalated and we ended up not speaking to each other for days, until she made the first move. She turned up at number nineteen with a bottle of *Blue Nun* and by the time we'd emptied it any disagreements were long forgotten.

'I'm sorry he's been bothering you,' I say.

'He's not bothering me, for God's sake. The poor bloke has lost a child and lost his girlfriend, all in the space of a few days and he doesn't understand why. You need to cut him some slack. Come to that, you need to remember that it was just weeks ago *you* lost a child.'

I change the subject and ask her about work and she tells me that Maria and Simon have split up after he announced he wanted to emigrate.

'He's off to Oz - thinks he's going to make it as a champion surfer or some such nonsense. I ask you. He

54

wanted Maria to go with him - give up her nursing career and everything. Trouble is, now she's desolate. I'm struggling to keep her from throwing in her job, she keeps threatening to go and work in *Top Shop*. My friends are all as daft as each other. Which I suppose says something about my choice of friends.'

Even allowing for the distance, I know she will be trying to form a picture of me, standing in a phone box, uncertain about my next step.

'Are you going to tell me where you are? Don't worry, I'm not planning to tell Mark, or send a search party.'

'I'm in Anglesey.'

'How did you end up there?'

'I don't know really.'

I take a deep breath and then I tell her, 'Gee, I've made a decision. I'm going to find my son. I need answers, however painful they might be.'

There is silence and I try to guess what she's thinking. Then she speaks and I can hear the smile behind her voice.

'I'm so pleased, Em. Really. And you know I'll be there for you, every step of the way.'

'There's something else. I've met a man.'

'You're a fast worker, sure you were only done with Mark five minutes ago. Now don't go making a mistake, take your time, there's no rush - play the field a while, you know what they say about loving on the rebound. I know I don't practise what I preach but...'

'It's not like that, he's...I don't know...there's something about him. He's homeless, at least, he works on the land. I don't even know his name.'

'Oh my Lord, you don't half pick 'em. What on earth are you doing with a down and out. You're successful, pretty - it's safe to say you could set your sights a touch higher than a vagrant.'

'No, listen. He's... I can talk to him, he's been through something and found a way to survive. He's younger than me, I'm sure of it, but he's learnt so much more about life.'

'Emily, you're not going all George Harrison on me - converting to Buddhism, swept up by a mysterious guru? You're better off joining a yoga group - at least there's safety in numbers.'

'My money is running out,' I tell her, as I hear the beeps on the line. I promise to ring again soon and vow to myself that tomorrow I will begin my search.

At first light I am in the kitchen. Ralph is still asleep, opening one eye, curious as to why I am disturbing his lie-in. I watch the birds circling above the sycamore tree that overlooks the front garden. They dip and dive, graceful and certain.

I make a second cup of coffee, prevaricating, apprehensive. This has to be right. I can't afford to make any mistakes. I take my notebook and open a double page spread. On the left I write:

Option 1 - Retrace my steps.
Advantages - I will find out first-hand what happened, how and when
Disadvantages - I will have to leave Anglesey and go back to Hastings

On the right-hand page I write:
Option 2 - Contact my parents
Advantages - I won't have to leave here
Disadvantages - Can I trust them to tell me the truth?

I start a letter.

Mum and Dad, I've decided to find my son.
I need your help.

I'd vowed I would ask them for nothing. I could start the search without them but it will take longer.

Please write and tell me where he was taken and who I can contact.

This is a business transaction. They have information I need, but they will want something in return. Me. They will want me. I need to provide an alternative because that is not an option. I am loath to give them a return address, although I know they will never venture this far north to track me down.

I consider Gee and the complications that could ensue if their reply arrived at number thirty-six. Worse still, I imagine the dilemma for Gee if my parents arrive on her doorstep.

I decide on a PO Box. The postmistress is happy to oblige and appears to have the discretion I'd hope for. As the letter drops through the slot of the postbox my mind fills with questions.

How long should I wait for a reply?
What if they've moved house? (extremely unlikely)
What if they choose not to reply?
How will I know if they're telling the truth? (Surely Mum's Catholic guilt would prevent her from lying, but is it a sin to withhold information? What would God have to say about that?)

There is nothing I can do now but wait.

Ralph and I walk across the headland most days. Sometimes the stranger is there and sometimes the bench remains empty. When we do meet him he's happy to talk and I find myself intrigued by everything he says.

Today it's a bright summer's day, with a strong wind blowing, making the clouds scud across the sky as if they are racing with each other. As we approach the cliff-top the wind is even stronger and in places I need to turn sideways into the wind to catch my breath. When we reach the bench Ralph's new friend is already there, sitting with his back to the wind. On his lap he has a sketch pad.

'Good morning, may I?' I say, pointing at the bench beside him.

'Be my guest,' he replies and shifts across a little to let me sit down.

'Looks as though it's you who is the artist,' I say, pointing at the sketch pad.

'Just messing.' He moves his hand away so that I can see his drawing, which is a beautifully detailed picture of a seagull.

'That's a lot more than messing, it's stunning. You have a real talent.'

'I wouldn't say that.'

'Do you sell your drawings? I'm sure you could.'

He laughs and shakes his head. 'Nothing like that, it's just a pastime. It's seen me through some difficult times. Shall we walk?' He closes his sketch pad and puts it into his rucksack. 'I'm guessing your young man here would like to stroll?'

'Seems he's decided you're his new best friend.'

'I'm honoured,' he says, as he bends to stroke Ralph's head.

'The view is magnificent from here, I can understand why you've chosen this bench as a favourite spot.'

'No boundaries, just the horizon. And the more I move towards it, the more it moves away.'

'This place shows nature off at its best, doesn't it?'

'Nature?'

'Yes, living here must make you really in tune with the countryside.'

'I've learned to be. There's usually work on all the farms hereabouts, picking crops, clearing fields, mending fences and in the spring I get to help with lambing.'

'And you live on the farm?'

'Home is a campervan, so I can park up wherever there's work.'

I have an image of his van, all his worldly goods around him.

'Is it just birds you draw?'

'I draw what I see. There are many ways of looking you know and many levels of seeing,' he says.

'How do you mean?'

'You and I might look at the same tree and see different things. I might see a chance for shelter from a rainstorm. You might see something that obscures your view, a lost opportunity to see the horizon.'

We walk a little further in silence. He picks up a stick and throws it for Ralph, but Ralph doesn't budge.

'He's lazy at heart you know,' I say, bending to give Ralph a gentle prod. 'He'll run if and when he's in the mood.'

'It's good to know your own mind, but I've found it can take a while to discover it. We might think we know about ourselves until we're faced with tough decisions. Then the self-doubt creeps in.'

'You should take up counselling.'

He laughs and strokes Ralph's head, rubbing just behind one ear, which makes Ralph look up at him adoringly.

'Most people have regrets about the choices they've made. It's just that some of us choose to own up to it.'

'You haven't met my mother. She has no self-doubt. She's controlling, opinionated and …' I look away, the colour rising in my cheeks.

'She'll have self-doubt alright, you just need to look closely, under the surface. Perhaps the truth is too complicated to explain. Perhaps it's not a series of facts, but a whole jumble of feelings. Maybe you need to look your mum in the eye to discover the truth.'

'You don't know her. In fact, you know nothing about me.' A rage builds inside me. Maybe the bottle of wine I worked my way through last night has done more than give me a thick head.

He smiles and holds his hand out to shake mine. 'All I'm saying is that I've discovered sometimes you have to turn things upside down to understand them.'

I know I should apologise, instead I bend to clip Ralph's lead on and stand.

'I'm Walter, by the way,' he says, before leaving us to finish our walk alone.

Chapter 9
Anglesey

This morning Miss Smart (who it turns out is called Laura Chambers) asked me to a Tupperware party. I am mildly surprised that Tupperware has found its way to this outcrop and even more surprised she considers me in need of some. But it's an opportunity to meet a few of the locals and do more than nod or say good morning and perfectly timed to provide me with yet another distraction.

I picture Gee's face when I confess I have purchased an unnecessary piece of plastic that will keep my celery crisp for days. I'm not even a great fan of celery. I vow never to tell her.

Laura's terraced town house is a short walk from the cottage and as I approach, I see I am one of the last to arrive. The lights shine out from the lounge where the curtains haven't been drawn. Eight or nine women are standing, in small groups of two or three, chatting and smiling. I recognise a few of the faces, but some are new to me. I ring the doorbell and am immediately welcomed into the hubbub. A glass of white wine is pressed into my hand and names are fired at me in quick succession.

'We'll test you later,' Laura says. 'Seriously though, don't worry, we don't expect you to remember us all. It's great you came though. We don't have many new additions to our little community. How are you finding *Martha's Cottage*? You could have brought your dog, I didn't think to say.'

Laura's chatter is a bubbling brook, continuous and refreshing. I'd been wrong about her occupation, although not too far adrift. Law is her profession, rather than teaching, which means Miss Smart still suits her well. I have to be careful not to call her that.

Questions are asked but no-one expects answers, the conversation flows, anecdotes are exchanged and family updates are shared. Penny Silver has twin daughters who have just completed O'Levels and are expecting great results. Felicity Archer is delighted her elderly mother has agreed to move in with her. Vicky Swindon's husband has been promoted and there's to be a celebration, to which we are all invited. Even me.

This is the ordinary life I have longed for. I imagine their faces when I tell them I have a child who I haven't seen since the day he was born.

'What about your parents, Emily, do they keep well? Are they far from here?'

'I've lost both my parents,' I say. It's a lie and yet it's true. Like Peter I expect to hear the cock crow three times.

I'm home by 10pm with an order placed for a set of Tupperware beakers I doubt I'll use and a miniature golf ball key-ring I won in the raffle. It's been a good evening.

Billy's lessons are going well and our Sunday walks are my chance to be crazy and childlike. I have been avoiding the clifftop walk since my run-in with Walter, so I'm pleased for any distraction.

'I'm really grateful,' Gwen says, when we return after our first Sunday walk. 'I've had a chance to do a bit of extra cleaning and get Sunday dinner ready. Usually Billy gets bored on a Sunday, kicking a ball out in the yard. It's family time for his friends on a Sunday, you see. It means they can't visit.'

I look forward to Sundays. I wake and start planning our walk as I grab some breakfast. Ralph is enthralled with his new playmate. Billy never tires of throwing Ralph a stick or a ball, or even retrieving it when Ralph can't be bothered.

'Shall I tell you a secret?' I ask Billy. It's our second Sunday walk and we're up a grassy outcrop that overlooks the beach. 'Ralph is lazy.' I keep my voice low and speak with my hand partly covering my mouth.

Billy looks at me wide-eyed. 'I won't tell, I'm good with secrets,' he says. 'But he's not lazy today, look at him run.' He takes off, running ahead, with an eager Ralph trying to keep up with him.

I still keep a diary and my Sunday escapades with Billy are the first cheery entries I've made in a long time. Gwen has asked me if I'd like to join them for Sunday lunch. I accept, but then wonder if it's a mistake. I could make a cake to take with me, but decide on balance that buying one is a safer bet. It's years since I baked and I'm still not confident with Martha's oven.

Billy, Ralph and I have our usual walk, but this time we're dodging heavy rain showers all morning.

'We should turn around now Billy, look at that black cloud,' I tell him as we approach the beach.

'Oh, no miss, let's not go back yet. Ralph loves the beach, we're going to race each other. Miss, you say ready, steady, go.'

Midway through the races the black clouds arrive over our heads and a deluge of rain beats down, bouncing off the pebbles. We run to a little beachfront shelter and wait until the worst of it is over.

When we reach Gwen's house Billy runs ahead, keen to tell his mum about our discoveries. We've collected shells on our walk and he's filled his pockets with them. As Gwen opens the door I realise I've left the cake at home.

'Hello you three,' she says. 'The kettle's on.' I see her face tense as she looks at Billy. 'You're wet through, go straight up and change.'

'The rain showers caught us,' I say, feeling the need to explain. 'We ran to a shelter as soon as we could. His anorak is pretty wet, but I'm sure it hasn't gone through to his shirt.'

'Billy knows he has to be careful. We ought to be used to the rain living here. Come through and have a cup of tea and I'll get Ralph a bowl of water.'

'I'm so sorry, I've forgotten the cake.'

I think about the reply that will take me forward to the next part of my life. I picture my parents' faces when they read my letter. I imagine their conversation. I wonder if there have been recriminations.

In the twenty years since I walked out of my childhood home I've been in contact with my dad three times. The first time was a few months after I left. I contacted him at work; he got a telling off from the factory chargehand for having a private call. I don't know what excuse he gave mum for making the journey to Brighton, but when I met him at the station and he put his arms around me, I was six again, my dad's little girl and all I could picture as he walked towards me was the day just after my sixth birthday when dad announced we were off for a treat. 'We're off to the fair, Emily, just you and me,' he said one day.

I couldn't decide what to be more excited about - visiting the fair with all its noise and strange smells, having the candy floss that dad had promised me - or having him all to myself, without mum to chide either of us.

I had a magical time, dad watched and waved as I went round and round in a musical teacup. He bought me the largest candy floss and laughed when I got it in my hair and on my nose. I marvelled at his aim as he knocked down a pile of cans to win me an enormous teddy bear and clapped when with just three balls we became the proud owners of a coconut.

Nothing was out of bounds that day. When I asked to go through the Tunnel of Death he looked surprised, but said he'd be right by my side. When the first monster appeared a few seconds into the tunnel my screams were of terror, not excitement. He took me in his arms and walked me straight out against the incoming flow of families. I clung to him tightly and hid my face in his jacket. Even now, when I smell Golden Virginia tobacco, I remember that afternoon at the funfair.

'Don't be scared,' he said, 'I promise I won't let anyone hurt you.'

The day I met dad on the forecourt of Brighton station I reminded him of the promise he'd made to me.

'How could you let her do it?' I asked him, watching his face crumple, the folds of skin around his jaw making him look like an abandoned dog.

'Come home, Emily,' was his reply.

We walked the length of Brighton seafront. He made me promise I'd keep in touch. When we parted he pushed a £5 note into my hand.

I cried more that night than I had for many nights. I wanted my dad to take away the pain, to undo all the mistakes I'd made, like rubbing out a wrong spelling with the simple sweep of an eraser.

Each day I organise my chores around a visit to the post office. Each day the postmistress sees me approaching and calls out, 'Nothing yet.'

Then one day she runs out of the post office, leaving a bemused queue of customers as she waves an envelope at me.

'You've got post.'

I try to assume a nonchalant expression while my heart thumps in my chest and my cheeks flush.

'Oh, thank you,' I say, as I take the envelope and put it directly in my jacket pocket. There's a hesitation as I wonder if she is expecting me to open it in front of her and announce my news. I smile and keep on walking, trying to focus on my footsteps.

Once indoors I take the letter and set it down on the kitchen work surface. I smooth it flat and look at the postmark. It's too faint to read, but I don't need to know where this was posted. The address is written in my mother's handwriting, it's unmistakable.

I imagine its contents. I make a pot of coffee. I want to know and yet...

Five times I go upstairs. I need another jumper. I've broken a nail and need an emery board. Endless diversions and each time I return to the kitchen the envelope sits, accusingly. *Why did you let this happen? Why has it taken this long for you to ask these questions? Why don't you open it now?*

I boil the kettle, refresh my cold coffee and take the envelope and my mug through to the sitting room. Ralph is asleep on his favourite chair and barely moves when I sit on the sofa beside him. I use a kitchen knife to slice through the top of the envelope. My dad always used his penknife. I wish he was here beside me.

Dear Emily…

I use a trick I used as a child when I was reading an exciting adventure book and I didn't want to know what was going to happen next. I use my hand to cover all but the top line of the letter and then slowly move it down line by line to uncover the news that will change the rest of my life.

Dear Emily

I've hoped for a letter every day since the day you left. Your letter told me that you are alive, but not what you are doing or where you are living. I hope you are happy.

There's a lot to tell you, Emily, but a letter is not the place. Do you think we could meet? I've read all your books and followed what little news appeared in the newspaper from time to time. From the articles I see that you are living in Brighton. Could I come to see you there? It's easy enough on the train.

I see that the PO Box address you've given for this letter is in Wales, which makes me think perhaps you're there for a holiday? Maybe I could come to see you in Brighton when you get back? There are things we need to talk about.

I have a telephone now so you could always ring me. I've written the number at the top of this letter.

I hope you will.
Love
Mum.

I want to take my coffee mug and smash it on the hearth. I want to scream. I will do neither because it would scare Ralph and spoil Martha's cottage.

Years and years of wanting to know and still nothing. My mother retains control and I am left with more questions. Hasn't she shown dad the letter? Why hasn't he signed it? Did she reply without telling him?

She's still making me play by her rules. She wants me to acquiesce - to a meeting, a phone call. Always on her terms.

I'm standing on a precipice, my balance is precarious. If I make one wrong move I will fall into the abyss. Perhaps I am already there.

'Come on Ralph, we need some fresh air.'

I grab Ralph's lead and put on my walking boots. I need a clear head to decide what to do next. As we walk, all the pictures in my head are of the day when I first left Hastings. I thought I was making a bid for freedom that day back in 1967 when I turned my back on all that had gone before, but now I know I can never be truly free until I know the whole truth about my son's life.

Chapter 10
Brighton
1967

In May 1967, Paul McCartney and the rest of the Fab Four sang, *She's leaving home, bye, bye*. I'd listened to the words over and over, lying on my bed, my ear pressed up to my transistor radio. Perhaps the song made me brave, or perhaps my own *'leaving home'* was inevitable. I walked out of my Hastings home before dawn one morning, and I'm certain that when dad found my note, carefully propped up on the mantelpiece, he would have said, *'Darling, our baby's gone'* or something similar.

I'd bought the train ticket a few days before. Since returning from the hospital, without the child I had given birth to, my bedroom had become my sanctuary. I'd retreat there straight after school, grabbing a sandwich and a mug of tea. There would be no more family teatimes, no weekend outings. The sign on the bedroom door telling them to 'Keep out' applied to more than my room; I wanted them out of my life.

The morning I left I scribbled a note and put it on the mantelpiece, propped up against a photo of the three of us. It just said, *'Need to move on. Stay well and try to be happy for me'*. They thought the cotton wool treatment would keep me safe, but it was too late for that. They didn't understand it hurt so much I couldn't breathe.

As the train pulled into Brighton station, the enormity of what I'd done hit me. I walked down the platform, gazing up at the vaulted roof; an expanse of glass and iron, grand and imposing. Around me was a hubbub of people coming and going. Porters wheeling trolleys laden with luggage; families chattering and excited; stylishly dressed men and women arriving and leaving. All so different from the day trippers who traipsed along the seafront of my home town of Hastings. Posters covering the walls of the station forecourt advertised the stuff of my teenage dreams: pop concerts, all-night dance clubs.

I walked out onto the main concourse and saw five or six groups of boys and girls, all around my age. It was like being on a film set. I'd seen some of the clothes in magazines, but here they were being worn, by people just like me. From the ground up there was excitement and controversy: the girls in go-go boots; coloured tights, miniskirts; plastic coats in yellow, black, white; and cute haircuts. The boys in Beatle boots and expensive-looking suits. I felt like a child in a sweet shop who has been told to look but not touch.

I watched the youngsters for a while; it was easy to merge into the background in such a frenetic place. Some of them drifted towards the station's exit and I followed. Once outside they mounted the Lambrettas that were lined up outside and sped off down the hill. With no other plan in place I decided to follow on foot. Ten or fifteen minutes later I arrived on the seafront. The wide expanse of the promenade, backed by elegantly decorated buildings, was a stark contrast to Hastings seafront. I wondered how two towns not that far apart could be so different.

A chilling north-easterly was blowing, but despite the temperature people were sitting on the beach. I spotted one family who were sharing a blanket picnic; they were laughing and taking it in turns to throw pebbles into the waves. The beach was lined with coloured beach huts, and along the promenade were Victorian shelters, a reminder of a bygone era. I found an empty one and sat looking out onto the wild sea.

Hotels and guest houses ran along the complete length of Brighton's seafront. I knew I had to venture into one, but wondered what I'd be asked. Would they want to know my age? My home address? Lies didn't come easily to me – my Catholic upbringing had seen to that – but make-believe was simple. Sleeping on the beach wasn't an option, so trying to think myself taller than my five-and-a-half feet and smoothing down my wispy hair, I walked up the steps of *Cherry View*. Mrs Lacey's uncertainty about whether to give me a room may have been overshadowed by the fact she had just one other visitor that week. When I felt the chill, both in the room and from her stare, I wasn't surprised. Nevertheless, I had a bed for a few nights at a price I could afford.

Fornication was not my only sin. I thought about how long it would take for mum to discover the empty tin. Each week she'd put a few shillings into the old Brooke Bond tea tin. It was no secret.

'We're saving for a rainy Christmas,' she'd say. The money bought our favourite extras. Dad's were *Quality Street* and redcurrant jelly; mine were marshmallows and lime marmalade. Mum said she didn't have any favourite foods. Her Christmas treat was for us to be together. It wasn't just the money I'd stolen.

The first night in Brighton I walked along the promenade. The lights on the West Pier were a blaze of turquoise, silver and pink, shouting out to all in the vicinity that there was fun to be had.

Over the next few days I walked past the *Zodiac Coffee Bar* three times before venturing in. The Vespas and Lambrettas parked up outside encouraged me, until finally I pushed the door and was enveloped with smells of frying and burnt toast. The floors were sticky with spilt coffee, trodden in and over, and the tables yet to be wiped. No-one looked up. Sgt Pepper was playing in the background. It was like going into a club where at last I understood the rules. Eyes were focused on newspapers, or their plates of runny eggs and crispy bacon, satisfying mind and stomach. Red and white checked plastic cloths covered the tables. I had to brush past wet coats hanging on the back of plastic chairs, to weave through to an empty table in the corner by the kitchen hatch.

'Share, if you like?' Her accent was familiar, reminding me of the Irish children I'd shared my schooldays with. She was long legged, with hair the colour of coal and her hand-knitted jumper a rich mix of red, yellow, orange, green and brown.

'You can't bag a table 'til you've got your drink – are you having a drink? There's no table service here, darling.'

Food and drink were an aside. After three nights in Cherry View, with Mrs Lacey showing clear disapproval at her young guest, I had to find a job and then a room. I'd escaped one regime and was loath to replace it with another.

'I'm Geraldine, by the way, but most folk call me Gee. And you are, let me guess...new in town?'

Two coffees later and Gee and I had discovered we were both Beatles fans, with the Stones coming a poor second. Our conversation was interrupted a few times with people coming over to chat to her.

'Tonight, Gee? *Leeroy*'s at 8?'

'Gee, meet you outside – don't be late.'

She laughed at my quizzical look.

'I appear to be their social secretary - well, that's fine with me – life's for living, that's what I say. Now, do you have a job? Somewhere to live? I don't even know your name.' Gee was direct and intuitive.

'It's Emily and no, neither to be honest', I replied.

'Okay, I'll be your fairy godmother if you like. When I arrived here I had to do it the hard way, trawl around the agencies, search the ads. But I can save you all that, can you type?'

'No.'

'No problem, my crowd are looking for a new junior assistant. They're a friendly bunch to work for, they'll send you to night school, they're great like that. How's your English, spelling and the like?'

'Pretty good.' She didn't need to know I sailed through my exams, despite the months of school I'd missed.

'Fine, well come along to this address at 10'o'clock tomorrow, dressed for an interview,' Gee said, shoving a business card into my hand. 'Do you have a skirt to wear?'

She told me briefly about *Black's Design* agency and reassured me I would love it.

'You'll fit in like an arm in a sleeve, or whatever the saying is.'

I wasn't sure there was a saying, or that I would fit, but I was in no hurry to question her. She was easy to talk to, for the first time in my life I felt like one adult speaking to another. I started to believe I could do this. If I felt daunted when I entered the café, my chance encounter with this charismatic Irish beauty meant I returned to *Cherry View* with adrenalin buzzing through me and this time it wasn't about flight.

It was only when Roger Black introduced himself that I realised he was the boss. He was the least likely boss imaginable and would have looked more at home on one of the Lambretta scooters that I'd watched parading around Brighton. At a guess I reckoned he was in his early twenties, his hair thick with natural waves, but close cut around his face and piercing blue eyes. A new Paul Newman film was due out and there were posters everywhere and now, here I was, sitting in front of his lookalike.

Roger asked me very little in the interview; was I prepared to work hard, that kind of thing. I remember nodding a lot, wondering why he kept staring at my knees. The skirt Gee had lent me was shorter than most of mine, but I didn't care. I'd left caring behind. She gave me a thumbs-up when I passed her desk on the way to the glass-fronted inner sanctum that was the boss's office. How long would it be before I looked as confident as she did then? She'd explained how she'd left Ireland a few years before. It was her portfolio of sketches and her artist's pad that got her the job at *Black's Design*, where she'd been ever since.

Within a week I started as junior assistant at *Black's*, which for the first year or so meant making teas and coffees and learning all there was to know about filing. I moved my paltry few belongings into the third bedroom of Gee's house share - thirty-six Cumberland Avenue - a double-fronted Victorian house, with a rusty gate hanging on one hinge, which I was scared to push too far in case the other hinge gave way. Either side of the path leading up to the front door were the remnants of daffodils that had finished flowering, with the leaves standing tall and looking hopeful. The door was dark green, glossy with fresh paint, which made me wonder about the gate.

As I looked for a knocker or a doorbell, the door opened to reveal a waif-like girl, her ginger hair in bunches and a red woollen scarf wound around her neck several times.

'You must be the newbie,' she said, 'your room's at the top of the stairs, second on the left. I'm Maria and I'm late. Must run, see you tonight.'

A few seconds later she'd disappeared around the corner. I remember feeling like an intruder. There was a creak on the stairs and I turned to see a tabby cat rush past me on its way to the kitchen, where the sink was hidden beneath a stack of unwashed mugs and plates.

'Welcome to you too, puss,' I said, 'I think I'm going to like it here'.

Maria was the third housemate. A student nurse who loved her nights out in her mini skirt and go-go boots a lot more than cleaning up sick and changing bedpans.

My room was next to the toilet, at the end of a narrow landing. There was a patch of damp in one corner, the ceiling wallpaper was yellowed and the bed looked as though it had recently been slept in. The small window looked out onto a back garden with a square of grass and some broken paving slabs.

Gee showed me her room later that afternoon.

'See what I've done with mine, you can make it as bright as you like with a few posters and paint. The landlord won't mind what colour. He's one of Roger's friends - your new boss - so he's easy.'

Most things were easy for Gee. My only decorating experience was watching mum and dad hang fresh wallpaper in the dining room at home, to discover they'd hung it upside down.

Gee helped me wash the paintwork, replacing the old net curtains with pink and black striped material we picked up at the Saturday market. She even knew how to sew.

'It'll be psychedelic in no time, you'll see.' We covered the old wallpaper in three coats of pink emulsion and painted the ceiling black.

'Stars, that's what you need,' she announced when we'd finished. 'Silver stick-on ones. Then you can lay back on your bed and you'll be looking at the night sky. Perfect, eh darling?'

Life had moved on. I wasn't a child anymore. I had a job and a room where I'd chosen my own colours, my own stars.

Chapter 11
Brighton
1967

Four nights in a row we'd fallen out of *Leeroy's* at 2am and sat in Fred's chip bar next door until he finally asked us to leave. Gee introduced me to pickled eggs and I'd introduced her to Merrydown wine, the cheapest way to get drunk. The combination meant an inevitable stop on the way home to be sick in the gutter. I was starting to get used to the room spinning as I laid my head down – a comfortable blanket of confusion before sleep.

The mornings were grim. We stumbled around each other, taking turns in the bathroom, hardly talking. Then one morning Gee waved three pieces of paper at me, while I stretched across her to put the kettle on for much-needed caffeine. The reality of it took a while to hit me.

'I've got them,' she announced. 'These three tickets will take us to Paradise, darling. Forget all your Hail Marys, music is religion for the soul.'

'Did you read that somewhere, or did you make it up? How did you get them – who did you bribe? Let me get to the kettle before I hug you.'

We'd heard about *The Who* concert weeks before, but there was little chance of getting tickets. Gee wasn't likely to tell us how she'd cracked the problem, but we didn't care. It was enough to know we would be there – as long as Maria could swap shifts and if she was prepared to leave Simon at home.

Simon made up our foursome and now there were just three tickets I could see trouble looming.

'Let's draw lots,' Maria suggested. She'd returned early from her shift.

'I thought you were on 'til lunch' I said. 'Have you been sacked? I'm not surprised, Holy Maria, you're a liability.' Gee's way of looking at things was rubbing off on me more than I realised.

'Calm down, I've not been sacked. I felt a little queasy and Matron said it was best not to spread illness and disease among the ill and diseased and she sent me packing.'

'Did you tell her the illness was courtesy of Fred's chips? Or did you play the poorly martyr?' Gee asked her. Gee's capacity for alcohol and comfort food meant she had little tolerance for those of us with more delicate constitutions.

Maria occupied the smallest room in our house share, which suited her, but wasn't fair when half the time she shared it with Simon. They'd met at *Victoria General* in Maria's first year. He'd fallen for her uniform and she for his porter's trolley. Their shifts often kept them apart, so when they were off together they came as a pair – rarely one without the other.

In the end we gave the third concert ticket to Suzy. She'd covered for Maria many times when she was late for a shift so we all thought she was owed a favour or two. We arrived at the *Dome*, four hours before the doors opened and were faced with five hundred or more people ahead of us.

'We have to be at the front,' Gee told us. 'Sharpen your elbows girls, we're in for the kill.'

We pushed our way through until we were close enough to the stage to believe Roger Daltrey was singing only to us. Guitar, drums and the screams of the two thousand crowd filled our heads. All around us fans were dancing and waving their arms around in a wild expression of excitement. This was living. It was raw, intense and free.

Four hours later we fell out of the *Dome* and linked arms as we walked home. The streets were buzzing, alive with the optimism of youth. Here anything was possible. I'd found all I wanted. Well nearly all. The job was fine, the company great and the dark times and nightmares less frequent.

I asked Gee once if she believed in God. It was a rare serious moment when we were walking over the Downs, heading for an ice-cream van, tempted by its melodic chimes, despite it being a cold spring day.

'I don't know what I believe in truth. What about you?'

'What about mortal sin? Do you think we're really damned from the moment we're born?'

She shrugged. There was a brief silence before she sought to lighten the mood with, 'Well, we may or may not have come into this world with sin on our souls, but we'll sure as hell make sure we leave it with some.'

For most of my childhood Sundays belonged to my mother and God. That meant donning my best coat, shined shoes and pocketing a clean hanky, then a march to St Thomas's. I never understood why we couldn't have breakfast first. The result was virtually every week I felt faint at some point during mass. The lack of food was compounded by the constant up and down, sitting and kneeling, which was required at specific parts of the service.

I heard all the words of the Mass, but listened to nothing. The monotonous drone of the congregation, their *'Amens'*, answering the unanswerable. Every week I repeated the words before taking Holy Communion, *'Lord I am not worthy, but only say the word and I shall be healed.'* As a child I hoped it meant my sore knee would soon get better, or my stomach would stop rumbling. Later, when mum was too ashamed to let me go to mass, she let me know how unworthy I was. I knew then that the concept of God's forgiveness only applied to certain misdemeanours; there would be no healing for me.

Now Sundays were sacrosanct in a way my mother would never have approved of. Around tea-time Gee and I would vie for the spot closest to the radio, listen to the chart show and dare anyone to speak when our favourite Beatles track came on.

My Brighton days, weeks and months drifted by. I was offered promotion to become secretary to Roger's business partner, Terrence Fortune, which meant more money. Terrence was a good boss, although his quick temper and my frequent typographical mess-ups meant we clashed now and again. After a while we settled on a truce, he eased up on the shouting and I focused a bit more. Plus the extra cash meant an upgrade to vodka and orange, which was easier on my stomach.

The owner of our favourite chippy had a heart attack, having enjoyed too many of his own fry-ups and Robbie stepped in. Chairs were taken from under us at 2am and placed on tables ready for sweeping. Enough of a hint for us to find another late-night venue.

I used some of my wages to treat us to a decent record player, which meant we started to come straight home from *Leeroy's* and work our way through the Bee Gees, Tamla Motown and, of course, our beloved Fab Four. We didn't have to worry about neighbours complaining –

they played Joni Mitchell and Dylan just as loudly and were comfortably oblivious in their smoky haze.

Some days I felt an ache deep within me. I'd lock my bedroom door, stare at my stars and try to imagine how it could have been. Those were the nights when the nightmare returned; the sense of desolation as the child in my dream was abandoned. My mother's words rolled over in my mind. *'You're too young, it's not right, it's not the way that God intended,'* I railed against a God who would allow a mother to be separated from her child. I railed against all religion, all rule makers, people who believed there was only one way to live and that was their way.

On many nights I sought oblivion. Alcohol was as far as I went to find it, we were offered other stuff many times – Simon had easy access to it – but Maria's horror stories of attempted suicides while under the influence scared us off.

Roger Black was making a name for himself among several of the trendy businesses. *Habitat* had approached the agency to pitch some designs for advertising and now Roger had been told that a selection of their designs were to be included in a London exhibition. He announced he would throw a party to celebrate, preceded by an extra day off. Gee and I spent the day preparing, painting nails, choosing lipstick. The word was there was to be dancing and free bubbly.

The previous Saturday I spent an hour and a few quid and watched as my lank locks fell to the floor. It felt good. Mum's regime of nightly brushing was ingrained into my psyche. I emerged from the hairdresser's and wanted to shout, 'Look at me, I'm free as a bird and there's nothing you can do about it.' But I didn't and even if I had there was no-one to listen who would have understood.

My dress for the party was perfect - a short, black halter neck with a white band around the bottom. Black kitten heels and a new clutch bag completed the outfit. Gee, always outclassing us, wore red hot pants and black knee-length boots. I'd guessed there would be photos and they would make it to the *Brighton Argus*. If my parents recognised their darling daughter, they would see how much fun I was having. Chances were they wouldn't. I didn't care either way.

'Had champagne before?' I asked Gee, as our glasses were refilled for the third time.

'No, and I still haven't. This is *Asti*, the cheap version, but who cares, it's bubbles. Feel it fizz up your nose. Em, I'm decided – I'll marry a rich man and live on a yacht.'

'Okay, I'll be your crew and scrub the decks.'

'You little scrubber, you'll do no such thing. Sure you'll have your own rich man, he'll whisk you off to Beverley Hills as like as not.'

The truth was I wanted none of it. I wanted what I couldn't have and the rest of it was a chance to forget.

The parties were fun, but drinking until I was sick in the gutter was not. Alan was now a frequent overnight visitor, sharing Gee's room and her sense of the ridiculous. He chatted her up the night of the awards evening, elbowing various others out of the running. My halter neck had attracted a few glances, but her hot pants had the desired effect.

'Let's go out on the pull,' she said to me one night.

'And Alan is where exactly?'

'I don't belong to him, Em, I don't belong to anyone.' Occasionally I could see a chink in her vibrant nature.

'Anyway, we have an open relationship and he likes me as I am, wild and dangerous.'

'Such an open relationship you're happy to cheat on him, and you'll turn the other cheek when he cheats on you?' I asked her.

'He's not like that, we're not like that. Oh hell, Em, I'm just talking about a giggle, nothing serious. Let your hair down why don't you – well you could if you had any left. By the way, I love the new cut, it makes you look like Twiggy.'

Looking back now, I can see how pointless it all was. I thought I'd grown up, moved my life forwards, when in reality all I was doing was standing still.

Chapter 12
Hastings

I came here to Anglesey to think. Now it seems that's all I have done. Too much thinking and not enough action. It's time for me to leave the cosy security of this place. I spend the early hours giving the cottage a final clean. I write Martha a *Thank you* card and prop it up on the kitchen table, beside a vase filled with bright sunflowers. As I turn the key in the door for the last time I wish there was another way. I've tried to run from my past when all I've done is taken it with me. Walter had said sometimes you need to go back in order to move forwards. When I close my eyes I see the possibilities that Walter described, but when I open them I see the darkness of the choices I have made so far. It's time for answers and it's my mother who needs to hear the questions.

Ralph senses the change in my mood. I told him last night that it would be our last walk to his favourite bench, the last hug with Walter. The only good thing about heading south is that I'll be closer to Gee. I rang her last night to explain.

'You've got your wish, I'm heading south again. I'm going to confront my mother - make her tell me the truth and after that, well...'

'One step at a time, Em. Anyway you've been up among the sheep for far too long. It's time you returned to civilisation - I'm missing my drinking partner. And before you ask, Mark has taken the job in Norfolk.'

I don't know if I'm relieved or sad.

'Norfolk's not that far you know,' she says. 'You can always visit. He's left me his new address but, Em, he's being brave, trying to move on with his life. Now it's your turn.'

Ralph is curled up on the passenger seat, ready for a long journey, six hours with a couple of stops. Six hours to prepare my thoughts, my questions.

The journey back is uneventful and as I reach the A21, each familiar landmark creates a sense of desolation. I had vowed never to return to this place where my life was upended irrevocably. And yet here I am, driving past the picnic sites of my childhood, past the house where my best friend, Sarah Wilton, lived. I wonder if the Wiltons are still there as I drive past their house, then down through the Old Town, past the amusement arcade with its flashing lights and piped disco music, enticing punters to spend their pennies and pounds. The paint on its frontage is still peeling, as is the decor on the front of all the Edwardian terraces, constantly battered by the winds coming directly off the English Channel.

'Don't you go near that arcade place,' was my mother's mantra. 'They'll take your money and give you bad habits for life. Gambling is a sin, Emily, remember that.'

Oh, I remember alright. The ten commandments are etched on my brain and I've tried hard in the last twenty years to break every one, apart from murder.

I originally planned to go straight to my parents' house, to avoid spending another sleepless night worrying. Instead, I'm too tired from the drive and Ralph needs a walk. Plus we need somewhere to sleep tonight and it certainly won't be under my mother's roof.

I park on the seafront and walk past the beach huts. A couple sit on one of the wooden benches, turned towards each other away from the wind. He unwraps the newspaper parcel that is on his lap and the smell of vinegar and fish wafts towards me. He picks up one chip at a time and offers it to her. Then she does the same for him, both of them laughing.

As I watch them I'm reminded of another picnic. It was our first day trip to Dover. Mum, dad and I caught the train, changing at Ashford, and made what felt like a long walk from the station to sit up on the white cliffs and watch the channel ferries heading out and coming home. Dad was excited, waving his arms around and pointing as each boat arrived and left, explaining about the engines and the funnels. I suppose mum had heard it all before because she took no notice, busying herself with pouring tea from a flask and unwrapping cheese and pickle sandwiches. I remember dad saying he'd always wanted to join the navy but was scared of being seasick, so he chose the army instead.

I've still got the photo (which must have been taken by a kind passer-by) showing my dad's animated expression, pointing out to sea. Mum and I sit beside him looking straight at the camera. I don't need to look at the photo to remember how misaligned we were; a family of three each with their own way of looking at the world.

I wander along the seafront, trying each guest house I pass. I call at a few before I find one prepared to let Ralph in. The first one I try is run by a woman who reminds me of my mother, her disdainful look makes me wonder how she attracts any customers. At the second one a robust and kindly looking man apologises and explains his daughter is allergic to dogs, otherwise he'd be delighted. At the third attempt a rosy-faced woman opens the door. She's short, stout and perhaps in her late sixties. Her face lights up when she sees Ralph.

'Hello, what a gorgeous dog you have there. He reminds me of my Charlie and it's a year to the day I had to say goodbye him, so that must be an omen. I miss him every day.'

Her gentle welcome is the perfect antidote to the angry thoughts I've had in my head since leaving Anglesey.

Ralph's tail wags in appreciation as she opens the door to the bedroom.

'The bathroom's down the hall, but you'll only be sharing with one other guest.'

'It's perfect, thank you so much.'

'How many nights would you like?'

With two nights booked and an open-ended invitation to extend should I need to, I nestle into bed. Ralph is still gently snoring as I wake. Mrs Caraway, or Tina as she likes to be called, greets me with a smile for breakfast and waves me over to the sideboard, which is covered with home-made delights; preserves, drop scones and freshly baked rolls.

'The muesli's home-made, as is the yogurt, but I'll admit to having bought the honey.' She chatters on as she goes back and forth to the kitchen through a swing door, arriving first with a pot of tea, followed by freshly laid eggs, perfectly poached.

I linger over the last piece of toast as I know the pleasure of breakfast will soon be replaced with bitterness and recriminations.

It's time. I've come here for this and the sooner I start the sooner it will be over. I park in Concordia Way, just around the corner from the house. I need time to gather my thoughts as I approach, but want the car to be close enough for a quick getaway.

With Ralph beside me I knock at the door. A few moments pass before the door opens. I wonder if she's out shopping and whether it will be my dad who greets me. I'm imagining his face, the joy in his expression and then the door opens and it's her. She looks at me for several moments. Perhaps she doesn't recognise me now that my lank mousy hair is cut and coloured into a neat blonde crop. And then she speaks.

'Emily.'

I stand and wait, not knowing if I want to be invited in, or if I'd prefer to turn around right now and flee.

'Emily, and...' She looks down at Ralph. 'Oh, I'm sorry but he can't come in, I've a cat you see.'

She's priceless. Twenty years on and nothing has changed. I turn to walk away.

'Wait, of course you can come in. Bring your dog too - what's his name? Just give me a second and I'll put Sparky up in the bedroom. He sleeps up there most of the day anyway, so it's no odds to him.'

We cross the threshold into a hallway papered with the same trailing ivy design that was there the day I left. I see the chips in the paintwork where dad dropped a vase and it broke against the staircase. Nothing has changed.

'Come into the sitting room. Have a seat and I'll put the kettle on.'

She stands hovering, blocking my way through.

'I can't believe you're here. I've thought about this day many times. It's wonderful to see you, Emily. You look well. Your hair, it's different, but very nice. It suits you.'

As I walk into the sitting room it's like walking back in time. My dad's favourite armchair is still beside the fireplace, with the coffee table next to it, but there's something missing. His tobacco tin isn't on the table. There's an emptiness about the room that makes me uncomfortable.

'Where's dad?'

As I ask her I realise I already know the answer. I can see it in her face. We stand side-by-side and look at dad's chair.

'Emily, I'm so sorry. I didn't know how to contact you. Your letter arrived just two weeks after the funeral. I wanted to tell you face-to-face. I couldn't have put it in my letter to you, it's not something you can write down.

Ralph lays down beside the armchair, sensing the need to be quiet and unobtrusive.

'What happened mum?' I ask her, although I'm not sure I want to know.

'It was very quick. A heart attack. The ambulance men came. They tried their best, but they couldn't save him.

Chapter 13
Hastings

Someone is shouting. The noise bounces around the walls of this empty room. Empty without my dad. I realise it's me who is shouting. I shout long and loud. I blame her for making his life miserable, for making my life miserable. I blame her for not telling me. How could she have had a funeral without his only daughter there to say goodbye.

She stares straight ahead, facing me but looking through me.

I fire questions at her, as I did when I was young. She says nothing. She never answered them then and she doesn't now. But this time dad's not here to help. He's gone and I am alone.

I leave the house and go back to the car. I slide onto the back seat, pull my knees towards my chest and let out a silent scream, squeezing all the breath from my lungs. Then the tears start to fall, running down my cheeks, my chin, my neck, until the collar of my cotton jacket is soaked. My nose runs and I attempt to swipe it dry with my sleeve, but then a second wave of grief hits me and all I can do is wait until my body has emptied all it needs to empty.

Throughout all of this Ralph has been lying quietly on the front passenger seat, as though he too senses the loss. After a while, I don't know how long, I crawl through onto the driver's seat, grab some tissues from the glove compartment and wipe my face and neck, tossing the wet tissues onto the floor. We drive to the far end of the seafront and park. I can't go back to the guest house yet, to be shut in with my thoughts. I need to find my dad. I need to revisit the places where he walked, the park where he pushed me on the swing, the beach where he showed me how to skim stones across the waves. I'm not ready to say goodbye to him yet. All these years I've chosen to abandon my dad and now it's too late, he's abandoned me. I dip my hand in my jacket pocket and pull out the only two letters my dad wrote to me. The first one arrived on my twenty-first birthday and the second when my first book was published. I replied to neither. I couldn't let mum know where I was; there was nothing I wanted to say to her that didn't involve anger and bitterness.

I don't need to read them, I've memorised every word. He wrote how much they missed me. And now he's gone I'll never be able to tell him I missed him too.

The next day at breakfast I know I still need answers from her, but I can't bear the thought of going back to the house, the last place where my dad was and is no more.

I spend some time walking around the memories of my childhood. My dad is everywhere, coming out of the paper shop with his *Daily Mirror,* his tobacco and those little packets of white paper for his roll-ups. He'd stand outside the shop, take out a piece of the delicate tissue from the packet, neatly place a roll of tobacco into it and then lick it down to make his own cigarette. My dad was never a drinker so there are no familiar pubs to walk past, but I can see him in all the cafés, enjoying his cup of tea and jam doughnut.

It was dad who opened up the world of words for me. I remember the first time he let me take his dictionary down from the bookshelf and set it on the dining table. A heavy book, full of mystery. The pages were thin, translucent ghosts of words - hundreds of pages and thousands of words with all their meanings. I'd challenge myself to read two pages a day.

'Awake' to wake from sleep; 'awakening' an act or moment of becoming suddenly aware of something.

I'd read them out aloud after supper and before homework and he'd listen. She'd be washing up and fussing around. My voice, or the nonsense of the unconnected stream often sent him to sleep, because before I'd finished the second page, *'azure' bright blue in colour like a cloudless sky; 'azygous' single, not existing in pairs*; my words were interrupted with the occasional snore.

My dad rarely got involved in parenting - that was mum's domain. He would sit quietly at meal times, only speaking to say, *'Pass the butter'* or *'That was delicious, Flo.'* Mum would talk throughout, recounting the events of her day, reminding us which feast day was coming next, or asking us if we wanted the leftovers made into meatballs or shepherd's pie. An endless stream of chatter, to which dad offered no more than a nod.

But I remember the day I came out of my bedroom wearing my first pair of jeans. Dad was sitting quietly in his favourite armchair, waiting for supper to be ready.

'No, Emily,' was all he said.

I railed. All my friends wore jeans, it was the fashion.

'That zip at the front is for a man, not a young girl. Go back to your room and put on a skirt, or a dress.'

It was the only time I can remember that mum was on my side.

'Leave her, Edgar, she wants to be like her friends. It's the thing nowadays, they're all wearing them.'

But dad had two sides to him, when Edgar and Flo were out and about, Edgar was in charge. His forceful announcements when we went into a shop or café were meant for everyone to hear.

'We'll sit here, Flo,' he would say in a booming voice. 'Emily - you this side, opposite me, and mother beside you. Now, what will you have? I'm having a toasted tea cake and a pot of tea.'

It was as though each outing was an unexpected adventure and he wanted the world to know about it. On a Saturday morning he would present himself in the kitchen, freshly shaved, smelling of Old Spice, with shiny shoes and a red handkerchief sticking out of the top pocket of his jacket. Mum would write a shopping list, check my hair was neat and tidy, and dad would stand quietly beside the back door, waiting for us. When we were ready he would open the door and my voiceless dad of my home life would become my noisy dad of the world.

Finally, I ring Gee, but saying it out loud will make it too real.

'Hey, there you are. Your timing is good, there are several parties coming up - all our friends are turning forty, Em. Time marches on, eh? Is my mate coming to see me?'

'It's my dad.'

'Oh, Em, I'm so sorry,' she says. She has always known without a need to explain. 'Is there anything I can do?'

'There's just her now. I've got to go back there and I can't bear the thought of it.'

'Maybe your mum will open up to you now there's just the two of you. She'll be grateful you're back in touch, maybe she's ready to give a little.'

I'm silent for a moment and then she says, 'Do you want me to come over? You sound like you could do with a hug.'

'I'll be alright.'

'Maybe you will, but a bit of moral support wouldn't hurt. I could be there in an hour or so.'

'Thanks, Gee, but I have to do this on my own. You're right, I need to go back and confront her.'

I put the phone down on Gee and then dial my mother's number before I can change my mind. It's strange to hear my mother's voice at the other end of a telephone.

'Mum, are you in later?'

'Will you stay for tea?'

'No. I mean, no food, just a cup of tea. See you around 4pm.'

Perhaps at last she will give me the answers I desperately long for.

Walking into the sitting room this time I take in the familiar surroundings in more detail. I imagine the delight of an interior designer, given carte blanche to transform this house that still represents past decades. The threadbare carpets would go, to be replaced with easy-to-clean vinyl or stripped pine flooring. Curtains would be torn down and instead Venetian blinds would dress the windows, letting through delicate shafts of light. Spotlights would shine in place of the faded lampshades that cover dusty light bulbs. But none of this would change the life my mother lives, or the way she sees the world. Not even rose-tinted spectacles would do that.

Ralph stretches out on the rug in front of the fireplace, his head resting on his front paws. Sparky has once again been consigned to the bedroom.

The ticking clock of my childhood, the one that told me it was time for school, for meals, for homework, has been replaced by a small gilt carriage clock that is chiming as I enter the lounge. I pick up the clock and notice the small plaque on the top and read the inscription: *40 happy years and every minute a treasured one.*

She comes into the room with a tray of tea.

'I bought the clock for your dad, had it engraved in Oakley's in Robertson Street. They did a good job, don't you think?'

My mother expressing emotion is new to me.

'We loved each other very much, Emily. I miss him every day.'

I can't talk about my dad, it hurts too much. I came here with one purpose, Thomas must be my focus now.

'Mum, the questions in my letter - you never answered them. I want to know where my son is. I have a right to know.'

'Shall I pour? Do you take milk?' She is precise in her movements, but I notice her hand shaking as she lifts the teapot. I wait and watch her as she sits down opposite me.

'Emily, it's all a long time ago and some things are best left in the past.'

'My son is not a thing, mum. I'm determined to find him and if you won't help me, then I'll find someone who will.' My voice is steady, but the anger is rising inside me.

'Why now, Emily? Your life has moved on. Your son will be twenty, he will have grown up in the only family he has ever known. Even if you could track him down all you will do is upset things.'

'Upset things? Oh, you're a great one for keeping things neat and tidy, aren't you? Don't upset the apple cart. Maintain the status quo. God, I wish dad was here, he'd understand.'

'Don't blaspheme.'

'Christ, mother. You have no idea what it's like. You took my baby from me on the day he was born and I can't go to my grave without at least knowing he's happy - that he's had a good life. Where did you take him, mum? Who did you give him to?'

I've disturbed Ralph with the rising pitch of my voice. He moves from his settled position on the rug and comes to sit beside me, his head pressing up against my knee, as if to provide reassurance.

She sets her cup and saucer down. Neither of us have drunk a drop. She stands up and I wonder what she's going to do. She goes to a drawer in the sideboard, pulls out a small brown envelope and hands it to me.

'You have a right to this, but I'm certain it will bring you pain, Emily. Some things are best left alone. Move your life forward, don't look back.'

I take the envelope, slide my hand inside and pull out a single folded sheet of paper. My mother watches me as I read it aloud:

St Joseph's, South Street, Brighton. This is to confirm that I entrust this child (parents unknown) to the care of St Joseph's. Signed Florence Carpenter.

The document is dated with the day of my child's birth. Within hours of me bringing him into the world my mother had allowed him to be disowned. *Parents unknown.*

Pictures flash through my mind. For years I lived four streets away from the place where my baby was taken to. The day I left and went to Brighton he would have been just a few months old, showing someone else his first smile, while I was out dancing with Gee. He was learning his first words when I started to create my stories. The pain is so intense it might be easier to cut off one of my limbs, at least then I would have a tangible wound to nurse.

She's still standing beside the sideboard, watching me, waiting for a reaction. I turn away from her, pick up the cotton jacket I'd thrown over the back of the sofa when I arrived and put it on, making my movements slow and controlled; the only thing left that I can control.

As I leave the house, with Ralph close beside me, she follows me down the footpath.

'Don't go, Emily, not like this. Let's talk. Let me explain how it was back then. There are things you don't know that will help you understand.'

I don't turn around as she continues to call to me. I keep walking until I can no longer hear her. I cross the road and go into the recreation ground of my childhood. It looks the same, but different. The roundabout has fresh paint, the gravel paths are covered with plastic mesh to stop children grazing their knees. The playground is empty. Children are at school at this time of day and dog walkers are banished from the play area. Rules and regulations to protect and control.

I find a dry patch of grass away from the trees and sit. I'm grateful for the solid ground beneath me. I let the tears flow. All the years of missing, all the regrets. Love that didn't have the chance to unravel, which never got started in the first place. Perhaps people pass by, if they do I don't notice them. My thoughts are in Brighton, inside *St Joseph's* children's home, imagining those early years of my son's life. The pain consumes me, I feel it at the very centre of me, the place where Thomas had nestled safely before he was born.

I've been sitting on the grass long enough to have lost sensation in my feet. I'd curled my legs up beneath me and now, as I stand, the buzzing sensation of the blood returning to my toes focuses my mind for a moment. Then I realise, I have an address, a focus, my search for Thomas can truly begin.

On the drive back to Brighton I'm grateful for the queues of traffic that delay me. I park in the shade, just around the corner from *St Joseph's* and leave the back windows of the car slightly open. I tell Ralph I won't be long, even though he pretends to be sleeping.

Once I'm standing in front of the imposing red-brick building, I look up at the three floors of small, leaded windows. How many times have I walked past this place, never knowing that Thomas was here, so close? If I had known I could have gathered him up and run away with him, far from Sussex, far from my mother's grasp.

I hover for a while on the doorstep and stare at the heavy oak door, wondering how many children have passed through it, how many families have been broken apart. Finally, I press the doorbell and wait. The door opens and I'm invited into a comfortable lounge, brightly furnished, with a TV and even a stereo system. Sister Angelica introduces herself, then walks ahead of me. Her hair is cut short and sits close to her head, no waves or curls to disturb the straight lines and no veil or covering. The familiar nun's habit is replaced with a plain grey dress, with a rosary hanging from around her waist. I watch it swing backwards and forwards, until she stops walking and turns to face me.

'How can I help?'

I hand her the paper.

She reads it and smiles. 'And you are?'

'I'm the child's mother.'

'Ah,' she says. 'Of course, this does say *Parents unknown* but either way, I'm afraid I can't help you.'

'Why is that exactly?' My cheeks start to burn.

'We don't have any of our records dating from those years. There was a fire you see, destroyed the whole of the west wing. Thankfully no-one was injured, but all our records were burned.' Her voice is steady, as though she has rehearsed the words many times. 'All the children who came to us were found good homes. If the boy is your son, as you say, then you can rest assured that he would have gone to live in a loving family who would have taken good care of him. I hope that helps.'

'Rest assured? I want to see my son, Sister Angelica, and there will be no rest for me until I know where he is and how he is. You have to help me.' Despite myself I grab hold of her hands. She pulls away from me.

'You are a little overwrought, Mrs Carpenter - it's best if you leave.'

'It's Miss. No marriage, see, no wedding ring. I'm one of those wicked, unmarried mothers. It seems God has many ways to punish. I haven't had to wait until the afterlife for my hell, I'm living it right now.'

The nun looks at me with horror and I wonder if she is expecting me to be struck down for such blasphemous thoughts.

'Don't worry, I'm going, but I'll be back.'

I turn and walk out of the room. I stride down the dark, soulless corridor and open a door that I think will lead me out. Instead I am in a bathroom, with a plain white basin and a toilet with a wooden seat. There is no mirror above the basin, instead I look at Jesus on the cross, with his head bent.

'Do you really want me to suffer for one mistake?' I shout at the inanimate crucifix. 'Aren't you supposed to be about forgiveness?'

I rip the crucifix from the wall.

Chapter 14
Brighton

Each route I've taken until now has been blocked. I need to find another road - an alleyway, or backstreet. I have the strangest idea a prayer could help. I had vowed never to set foot in a church again after my mother's God encouraged her to steal my child from me. But now I need to reach out to something beyond this world of closed doors, blank looks and lies.

The library was often my sanctuary when I needed to think, gaining comfort from being surrounded by books that offer an escape into the worlds of others. I push the swing door and enter the stillness, a church that doesn't preach or interfere. The librarian looks up briefly as I enter, before returning with a look of concentration to the microfiche. I walk along the aisles, and stop to look through a small section headed *'Spiritual'*. Perhaps another God can provide some answers. I select a book and find a corner seat. Undisturbed I read through the chapter headings and think about Thomas, that part of me out in the world with whom I am connected but to whom I have no connection. Until now the search has always been mine, but today I realise perhaps he is also searching. If I reach out maybe the Universe will help me.

I haven't told Gee I'm in Brighton. I wanted to surprise her, to arrive at her door and announce my discovery. Instead I have no discoveries to announce.

I knock on the door of thirty-six Cumberland Avenue and then notice the shiny new bell push with instructions to 'press me' written above it. I press it twice and hear a three bell chime ring out. Within seconds the door opens and her smile reaches from her mouth to her eyebrows.

She holds out her arms and pulls me in, with Ralph getting caught up between us.

'Am I pleased to see you. And you're just in time. Roger and I are having an argument about whether there is any point to decaffeinated coffee. You're on my side? Of course you are.'

She hugs me so tight the breath is squeezed from me and then she holds me out at arm's length.

'Let me look at you. Oh, my word, you've lost weight. Toast is what you need, followed by lunch at Mario's. Mario is our new best friend, he makes the best spaghetti carbonara this side of Venice or wherever it hails from. God, I've missed you. Why didn't you ring to tell me you were coming? Are you staying? Of course you are.'

If I had a sister I couldn't love her any more than my wonderful friend. I let her lead me into the kitchen and ply me with toast and coffee.

'Do you want to talk about it?' she says, as we sit opposite each other at the kitchen table.

'I don't know where to start'

'It must have been such a shock, the news about your dad.'

'That wasn't the only shock.'

She stretches her hand out to hold mine and I tell her about my visit to *St Joseph's.*

'Dear God, Em, these people with their sanctimonious, self-righteous, religious, claptrap.'

'Don't hold back,' I say and she laughs.

'Seriously though, what gives them the right to stand in judgement? It makes me sick to think about it.'

'They live their lives by a rule book, it's called the *Bible.*'

'Rubbish. Where does it say in the *Bible* that it's okay to take a child from its mother and then lie to her when she's desperate to find him. It's all about control.'

'Let's not talk about it anymore. Tell me something nice. Anything.'

She takes a deep breath. 'Okay, well, Maria didn't pine for Simon for long. She's met a new fellow, jacked in her job and they've gone off to some far-flung place on some volunteering project. I ask you. One postcard is all we've had. They say they're working hard, but can you really believe them? And then there's William - you remember Wills from *Black's*? Always thought he was more important than the rest of us just because his dad had a country estate or some such rot? Well he's been sacked. Poetic justice, or what? Apparently there was talk of him fiddling his expenses - and him with all that money. *Flash with cash* we used to call him, do you remember? Just shows you, you never really know a person.'

I could listen to her forever. Her voice washes over me, bathing me in calm and positivity. With Gee beside me I can move mountains, if that's what it takes.

A couple of hours later we wander aimlessly around the Lanes. We stop for a while listening to a busker, with a cap placed conveniently on the ground for offerings. He's strumming a guitar and is so absorbed in his music it's as if he hasn't noticed the small crowd gathered around him. He's maybe twenty, clean shaven, blue jeans and a white tee-shirt. He could have merged into the crowds unnoticed, but for the guitar in his hands.

'He's good,' Gee says. 'Who knows, maybe one day he'll be famous and we can say we saw him before he was discovered. Just like you, Em. I wonder if fame will change him, if he'll take to it. You never have, have you my little wallflower. Now if it was me, I'd be shouting it from the rooftops: *Look at me, I'm famous.*'

Some of the people who had been listening to the guitarist turn to look at us.

'You've done it again. Come on, let's get out of here,' I say as I tug her arm and pull her away from the crowds.

'Does your Walter busk?' she asks me as we stroll arm in arm towards Mario's.

'He's not my Walter.'

'You know what I mean.'

'He works on the land, on farms, that kind of thing.'

'But does he play an instrument? Next time you see him tell him that's the way to go.'

'He whistles.'

'Whistles?'

'Yes, he can copy pretty much any bird whistle he hears, and anyway, who says there will be a next time?'

'Your mate does. The one who can see inside your very soul,' she says smiling.

Mario welcomes us as though we are his old friends.

'The best table for my best customer. Are we eating? Or is it just a fine *Valpolicella* with some olives for you today? I can recommend the *pesce* or Mario's special *spaghetti marinara.*'

We decide on salad, olives and garlic bread and a bottle of the house red. By the third glass I am starting to feel a bit better. I ask her about Roger and she giggles like a schoolgirl.

'Who knows where it will end, but for now it's good, I'm having fun. But listen, Em, I've had an idea.'

'Okay, go on then.'

'How about you contact your agent?'

'Why would I do that? She'll just moan at me because I've not written anything in months.'

'I'm trying to think of ways to get you some publicity. I know you're a private soul, you don't want the world knowing your business and I don't blame you.'

I pick up an olive and roll it around in my fingers, then put it down on my plate, uneaten.

Gee continues. 'Do you remember that girl - the one who interviewed you? All pink and perky was the way you described her, wasn't it? Why not get in touch with her, tell her your story? Out there somewhere is your boy, so what better way to find him than to use the press? Turn the tables - it'll make a change, they've used and abused people often enough for the sake of a cheap headline...'

'I know you mean well, but I don't think I can stomach it. They'll twist my words and before I know it I'll be portrayed as an evil bitch who gave her child away and then went on unfettered to fame and fortune.'

'Hm, okay, let's think about it. Perhaps there's another way.'

There wasn't another way, or at least if there was one we couldn't work out what it was. The next morning I return to the library to check whether Jocelyn is still working for the *Daily Herald*. I find her byline under an article about a national awards evening and make a note of the phone number, find the nearest phone box and call her, before I lose my nerve.

'Jocelyn, it's Emily Carpenter. You interviewed me for the *Daily Herald*.'

'It's good to hear from you. I'm not sure my editor is looking for any author biogs at the moment, but I can always let you know when he is.'

'Thanks Jocelyn, but this is one author interview your editor will be interested in. So interested in fact I'm prepared to give you exclusivity. All I ask is for it to be a main feature, not shoved into a column somewhere on page twenty. Pitch it right and this story will get you noticed, Jocelyn.'

It was the word 'exclusive' that provided the hook, maybe she could suddenly see the chance for promotion - taste it even. She didn't say anything for a few seconds and then, 'Just tell me when and where - I'll be there.'

Now I have to prepare to remove the protective layers from around my life and lay it out for the world to see.

With Gee and Roger at work, Ralph and I have the place to ourselves. They've convinced me to stay for a while and I'm back in my old room, the psychedelic colours and starry ceiling replaced with muted pastel furnishings and matching curtains.

Jocelyn rings the doorbell and uses the knocker - she's still as keen as that first time we met, buzzing with anticipation.

'Emily, it's good to see you.'

'Thanks for coming. Would you like a drink? Hot, cold, tea, coffee?'

'Just a glass of water, thanks.'

She is nervous and yet it should be me who is quaking. I remember her vibrant pink nails and lipstick from our first meeting. This time she's wearing a short navy dress and a neatly cut square edged jacket. Her hairstyle is unchanged, but she looks younger than I remember her.

She hovers next to the dining table and I gesture to her to sit. 'How's the writing going? You were hoping to try your hand at fiction, weren't you?'

'Oh, I've played around with a few short stories, but to be honest I'm not sure I'm good enough. Journalism requires writing skills for sure, but fiction - well, you need a vivid imagination and that's never been my strong point.'

'I'm sure you've got it in you, you just need to persevere, the ideas will come if you let them.'

'You're very kind, but that's not why I'm here. You mentioned on the phone you had a story to take my breath away.'

'I'm not quite sure that's how I described it, but yes, I have something to create a few shockwaves among your readers.'

'And you're offering me this as an exclusive - is that right?'

'Yes.'

'Why? I mean, why me?'

'I've spoken to you before and I trust you to deal with it sympathetically. It's a difficult story to tell and I only want to say it once.'

'Well, thank you. I mean, thank you for trusting me. I'll do my best to make sure your story gets the treatment it deserves. I've told my editor I'm meeting with you today, he's keen to know more and he's very supportive. I'd like to think you've chosen well by trusting us with this.'

Now the moment is here I'm not sure how to start. I don't even know if I want to. I get up and go into the kitchen - it's my turn to need water. I sip it and try to calm myself.

'Do you mind if I record this interview?' she says. 'I'll make notes, of course, but a voice recording would be best - if you don't mind?'

I nod. If I am going to be taped I will have to choose my words even more carefully.

Jocelyn is sitting with her pencil poised and the tape recorder is blinking a red signal.

Chapter 15
Brighton

The article has been out two weeks and the letters are arriving daily. I can't bear to open the envelopes, so I let them pile up. Gee doesn't mention them but they stare at me from a wire basket on the kitchen worktop while I have breakfast or make coffee. I imagine their contents - accusing diatribes of parents who will no longer allow their children to read my books, others indignant that I was allowed such freedom and abused it, let my parents down. I prepare to hang my head in shame. I have sinned and the contents of these letters will confirm I don't deserve forgiveness.

It's Saturday morning and we've had a lie-in.

'Where's Roger this morning?' I ask her at breakfast, as I sit ready to eat toast and marmalade.

'He's taken up jogging, worried I'll show him up on the fitness stakes, him being so much older than me,' she winks at me and then grabs a handful of the letters that have piled up, reaching the top of the basket. 'Okay, I've been patient and I know what you're worrying about, but until we start working through these we won't ever get any further forward. There are two options - either I open each one and read it out to you, or we open one each. What do you think? I'll be beside you every step of the way, Em. You're not alone and I bet it won't be as bad as you think.'

I watch her as she makes two mugs of coffee and sets one down in front of me. I push the toast away.

'I've messed up well and truly this time, Gee, I should never have given that interview. Why did I imagine for one moment it would help? People will always want to think the worst and I've given them plenty of ammunition. I'm finished here, perhaps I should move abroad - south of France, Italy maybe - or further. It could be fun.'

She glares at me but doesn't speak, so I continue. 'If my selfish mother had thought more about my child, rather than her own religious bigotry I might still have him. Instead I've had to open myself up to anyone who wants to judge me.'

'You should listen to yourself, Emily. I love you dearly but you can be so blinkered. Life's not simple, people mess up. Your mum would have had her reasons for doing what she did and I doubt that one of those reasons was to hurt you. You've tried and convicted yourself without any defence - no jury even. Do you really think you're the only person to have made mistakes? Get a grip, the trick is to pick yourself up, dust...'

'I know the song well enough. I'm not as brave as you.'

'Oh yes you are, my friend, every bit as brave. Okay, here goes, here's the first one - picked at random. The handwriting is friendly, don't you think?'

I smile, despite myself. I doubt how much could be determined from a hastily written address on an envelope, but she's right, it is time.

Dear Emily,' (the letter reads) *'I've read all of your books to my children, several times over. Some of them I know by heart. I was very sad to read the article in the Daily Herald about the terrible experience you had having to give up your child. I have two children and I feel blessed every day.*

Gee stops reading and puts the letter down beside me.

She opens another and starts to read.

Dear Emily, I can imagine how you must feel. I also had to give up my child. My parents were understanding but they had no money and life was difficult enough for us as I was one of five. I think about my child every day.

Her voice peters out and I look up to see her wipe her face.

'What?' she says defensively. 'I'm pretty sure I have a cold coming. You read the next one.'

We work our way through a dozen or so and take it in turns to tear pieces from the kitchen roll that sits on the worktop beside us.

'Not a cold then,' I say quietly.

'All these lives, Em. So many women had their lives disrupted because they didn't play by rules that were created centuries ago - it's all such a wicked waste.'

The toast remains uneaten and the coffee untouched. We continue through a few more letters, by which time Ralph is demanding my attention.

'Are you coming for a stroll with us?' I ask Gee, expecting her to decline as dog walking has never been her favourite pastime.

'Do you know, I think I will. Time to clear our heads and get rid of these colds,' she says, smiling.

The wind is brisk and the waves crash confidently onto the shingle. A crowd is gathered around one of several ice-cream kiosks that line the seafront. We watch as a little girl with perfect pigtails elbows her way through to the front of the queue.

'She'll do well in life,' Gee comments, 'I like her enterprise. A business woman, or even a politician?'

A woman moves forward and takes the child, guiding her back to her place in the queue. She bends down and speaks quietly to her.

'The art of gentle persuasion,' Gee says. 'A good lesson for a child who is destined for great things.'

'You should be the writer,' I say, 'you've written her life story and she can't be more than five.'

We walk to the far end of the promenade and let Ralph pull us down onto his favourite part of the beach where he can chase the few pebbles we throw into the water.

'Have you thought about what you'll do if he gets in touch, Em?'

She's asking me a question I have asked myself every day since I left Mark. I'm no closer to the answer.

So many of the letters tell of the hardships endured by young mothers who either weren't allowed to keep their child, or who had done so and found the struggle of daily life almost unbearable. I am reminded of Gwen and Billy and decide to phone.

'Hello, Mrs Davies, it's Emily, Emily Carpenter. I thought I'd ring to say hello to Billy, see how he's doing with his English. I know it's been a while.'

There's silence at the other end of the phone. I freeze. Billy has died and it's my fault. His pneumonia must have returned because of that day we got soaked in the rain. I sit on the floor, put the receiver down beside me as I double over with guilt.

Then I hear a voice, shouting at me. I pick up the receiver and hear him say, 'Miss Emily, hello, it's Billy. Guess what Miss, I came second in spelling last week. Mum cried. I think she was happy though. I got a star and Mrs Cranmer said she was very pleased with my progress. Miss, what do you think? That's good, second place, isn't it?'

I wipe away tears and try to steady my voice.

'That's great news, Billy, you should be really proud of yourself. I'm so delighted, well done. Billy, can I talk to your mum a minute? Keep up with those spellings, won't you?'

Gwen's voice is tentative.

'Hello Emily. As soon as I heard your voice I thought I'd call Billy, let him tell you his good news. I'm so grateful for all you did for him. And Emily, I hope you don't mind my asking, but when you were here we didn't put two and two together. What with Billy not reading many books back then. But since you left we've got two of your books from the library. Now Billy keeps telling everyone he knows a famous author. I'm quite embarrassed, we didn't realise. '

'Let me stop you there,' I interrupt her, 'don't worry about it. I'm not a great one for fame and all of that. I've just been lucky, as far as my writing goes.'

As I continue to talk to her I wonder if she saw Jocelyn's article, what she would think about a mother who let her baby be taken from her, whether she'd feel pity or disdain.

'Gwen, I must leave you to get on, but I'll ring again to say hi to Billy. I'd like to keep in touch, if it's okay with you.'

'Oh yes, we'd be delighted. You should see Billy's face now he's told you about his progress, he's beaming from ear to ear. Don't leave it too long before you come to see us and Billy says to please say hello to Ralph. He misses those walks. He's made me promise if we ever get a dog it has to be as special as Ralph. A bit of a tall order.'

Roger has taken to running every evening after work, so each day before supper we open the post, with a glass of wine to still our nerves. There have been a few letters that reprimand and sling the kind of insults my mother would approve of, but many of them just want to share their stories of love and loss.

Gee curls her long legs up beneath her. She plumps up one of the cushions and puts it behind her back.

'I used to be able to get comfier on this sofa, but now everything feels stiffer.'

'Welcome to middle age.'

'The letters are depressing enough, without you adding insult to injury. Why did we decide to read these? Remind me.'

'Because you're my best mate and you drew the short straw in the friend stakes - choosing a loser with too much baggage.'

She straightens up and puts her feet down on the floor. She looks away from me towards the window. It is twilight and the lamppost across the street is starting to come on, casting a flickering orange light across the front of the house.

'Maybe pull the curtains,' she points to the window.

'Yes, madam, straightaway.'

'No, I'll do it.'

'Where have you gone? You're off in a reverie somewhere - can I join you?'

'You wouldn't want to, trust me.'

She goes into the kitchen and returns with a bottle of *Valpolicella*, a corkscrew and two glasses. She is quiet as she opens the bottle and pours us each a glass. She hands me one of the glasses and stands looking at me, but I get the sense it's not me she's seeing.

'We're a messed-up generation, Gee,' I say, topping up our glasses. 'Weren't the sixties supposed to be about free love, give peace a chance and all that? How come there's all this collateral damage?'

'People are scared of change, and it always ends up with the women suffering. Look at Pankhurst and what she and her mates had to go through just to get us the vote. Men were terrified we'd have an opinion, do things better than they could. Not much has changed since then if you ask me.' She smiles and takes a long drink.

'You're right about fear, my mother was terrified of disobeying the church - I'm sure she believed her God would strike her down. And dad, I think he was just scared of mum. I miss him.'

She reaches her hand out to me and for a while we are both lost in our thoughts.

'Dad was a gentle soul. I'm sure mum bullied him into agreeing with her. I wish I could talk to him now, adult to adult.'

'We don't know what goes on in a relationship, Em. Chances are they loved each other very much, but I expect they'd fallen into a pattern. Perhaps your dad found it easier to agree. Anything for a quiet life and remember, they probably have their own demons, stuff in their past they had to deal with.'

'Top marks for diplomacy and forgiveness. You might be right, but on the other hand...'

'Okay, time for us to eat. We don't need to wait for Roger, he's going to the pub with his running club. A chance to undo any good he might have done.'

We work our way through one of Gee's signature dishes, her own take on an Irish stew without the meat.

'You're on washing up,' she says. 'And then let's curl up and listen to music.'

We take it in turns to choose a favourite album. By the third record the wine is finished and Gee suggests a second bottle.

'You have work in the morning. I don't. So, it's your call,' I say.

Chapter 16
Hastings

Gee has persuaded me to visit my mother again.

'If you can't make peace with her, Em, at least try to declare a truce. Give her the chance to explain. She's just human you know and we all make mistakes.'

'Not my mother,' I say, 'you don't know her.'

In the end I agree to go over for the day.

'But I'll be back by the evening,' I tell Gee, as she's making a shopping list.

'What shall I get you for supper?'

'Nothing, don't worry, I'll make toast if I'm hungry. I have the feeling the day will take away any appetite I might have had.'

'Don't be such a pessimist,' Gee says, without looking up from the list. 'Shall I get bacon? Oh no, I forgot. You don't, although don't think I haven't seen you drooling over my bacon sandwich.'

My mother doesn't ask me any questions when I ring. She sounds hesitant. I wonder if she is preparing herself for another confrontation.

'I'll be there at midday tomorrow, but I won't stay long,' I tell her.

'You might have to change trains - the Saturday service can often be disrupted with engineering works. Don't worry if you're late. It will be good to see you, Emily.'

She is right about the engineering works. By the time I reach the house it's nearly 1pm. She opens the front door almost before I've knocked, as though she's been hovering in the hall.

'Emily, you look well. Come in, I've got the kettle on. Tea?'

I want to dispense with the niceties, the small talk and get straight to the reason for my visit. I follow her into the dining room, watching the back of her mule slippers slipping up and down each time she moves. I'm certain I remember the tweed skirt, blouse and cardigan. Can it really be the same one she wore twenty years ago?

She sits down on one of the upright armchairs and gestures to me to sit down next to her, but instead I pull over a dining chair and sit opposite. She puts her hands in her lap and starts to fiddle with a cotton thread that is loose at the bottom of her cardigan.

I wonder which of us will speak first - who will be brave enough to raise the subject that has created a chasm between us for twenty years.

'Emily,' she says.

'Mum,' I say at the same time. We both smile. A little of the ice has broken.

'You first,' she says.

'I don't want to talk about dad.' The pain is still too raw and part of me wants to pretend he is just out for a walk, that perhaps I'll see him later. 'It's Thomas I'm here to talk about. Since I saw you last I've been to *St Joseph's* and they told me precisely nothing, on the pretext that all their records were destroyed in a fire. Excuses I'm sure, but I've spoken to a journalist, she wrote an article.'

'I know, I've read it.'

'Then you know the lengths I'll go to find him. I've opened up my private world to strangers in the hope that Thomas will come out of the woodwork. But nothing, just nothing.'

'Did you receive many letters?' she asks.

'I did as it happens. Plenty. But none from him. Although I suppose it was always going to be a shot in the dark. He may not even know he was adopted.'

'What did the letters say?'

'All kinds of things - people who had been in the same boat as me. Some who had been adopted and had tracked down their birth mother. A few who just wanted to sympathise with me, who genuinely seemed to understand. A couple who wrote that I should be ashamed of myself. Why, did you think they would be full of hellfire and brimstone?'

'I wrote to you, Emily.'

'Pardon?'

'One of the letters was from me. I changed my name, of course, and wrote it all in capitals to disguise my handwriting.'

She's looking at me as she speaks, but then she looks down at her hands again and continues to play with the loose thread.

'Did you write to tell me again how wicked I was, how the Lord will never forgive me and how I need to seek repentance?'

'Shall I make tea?'

'Will you stop worrying about the blessed tea and tell me what you're on about?'

'Emily...' she stops and stands up.

'Where are you going now?'

'I'm just going to fetch something,' she says. I hear her climb the stairs and go into her bedroom. There's a rustle of paper and then she's down again with something in her hand. She gives it to me. I open up the tissue paper parcel to find a baby's bonnet, finely embroidered, the ribbon is yellowed. I hold it in my hands. I caress it. I form a picture of the tiny head that once lay within it.

She sits down on the same armchair and looks directly at me.

'It's not your son's,' she says.

A few moments ago I felt closer to him than I had felt for twenty years and now she's taken him away again.

'I won't play your guessing games, mum. If you have something to tell me just come out with it. If not, I'm leaving. I'm not sure I should ever have come.'

She takes the bonnet from me and lays it in her lap. Her fingers run over the edges of the bonnet. She is caught up in a reverie, I wonder if she even realises I'm there, sitting across from her, holding my breath, waiting for her to explain.

'Your dad and I…'

'I'm not sure I want to hear this. You can't blame dad for something when he's not here to defend himself.'

'Emily, please hear me out. I should have told you this long ago. But you were just a child, and then as soon as you were all grown up you left.'

I stare at her hands as she plays with the ribbon of the bonnet, winding it around her fingers.

'Your dad and I loved each other very much,' she continues. 'We knew right from the start we wanted to marry, but I was still so young. I was just eighteen and my parents, well, they wanted us to wait until I was twenty-one. Times were different then. Anyway, I knew nothing about the ways of the world and one thing led to another. The thing is I found out I was expecting a baby.'

I gasp, but before I can say anything, she continues.

'Don't stop me now. I need to keep going or I'll never get it out. Edgar was as shocked as me. We decided to tell my parents together, to explain how we loved each other and we wanted to get married. But they told me to leave, pack my bags there and then. We didn't have any money, it was wartime. We didn't know what to do or where to go. In the end his parents said I could share his sister's room - Auntie Violet - do you remember her?'

I have a vague image of a rosy-faced woman, with my dad's hazel eyes.

'She came to visit just the once when you were a toddler. It was a difficult weekend. She and your father had a row and now for the life of me I can't remember what it was all about. Anyway, she left a day early, packed her bag and left before breakfast.'

She fidgets in her chair and for a moment it's as though she's forgotten where she is or what she was saying.

'Mum, the baby - what happened?'

'Your dad's parents said I could stay until the baby was due and then I was to move to the *Convent of the Rosary* - it was a place for unmarried mothers, run by nuns.'

She pauses, perhaps she is expecting me to say something, but I remain silent.

'I stayed at the Convent just three weeks. They gave me two days to hold my daughter and then they took her from me. They had a couple all lined up ready to adopt her. I wasn't allowed to meet them. I left Charlotte in her crib and went out one door, and the couple came in another door and took her. I never saw her again, but I still remember her tiny fingers, their tight grip.'

Her head is bent and her voice has become more quiet until it's almost a whisper. She takes a handkerchief from her skirt pocket and wipes at the corner of her eyes.

'I know what you're thinking.'

'I doubt that, mum.'

All that I have known until this moment is unravelling. I'm standing on shifting sand, whichever way I move, I'm certain I'll sink.

'You're wondering how I could have put you through all that pain when I know how hard it would be, when I'd had the same experience. But that's just it you see. I wanted it to be different for you. We would have…'

'What would you have, mum? Forgiven my sins? It wasn't forgiveness I wanted. It was understanding. You of all people should have known that.'

'I made a mistake.'

'Which mistake are we talking about mum? Handing over your firstborn child or making me do the same with mine?'

'You're very angry aren't you? Still so very angry.'

She looks at me.

'I don't know you anymore. You've made your own way in life. If you'd had a child to support, your life would have been different, it would have been hard.'

'You're the stranger, mum.'

I'd left Ralph with Gee, but now I wish he was here with me, providing a different focus, helping me breathe.

'Let's make that tea,' I say.

She follows me into the kitchen. She looks so small, so vulnerable. I try to imagine her at eighteen, falling in love, allowing passion to tempt her to break her precious rules. I wonder what my dad felt about it, whether anyone gave him the chance to choose.

'Do you know where she is now? My sister?'

'I was never brave like you. I've never tried to find her, but I think about her every day, wondering if she's happy. I might even have grandchildren.'

The irony is a kick that winds me.

'You do have a grandchild, mum, remember?'

On the train journey home I look through the window and see nothing for a while. My eyes are open but my mind is closed to anything but my mother's words, which I repeat over and over. I wonder how hard it was for her to tell me her story. Perhaps she thought it would help me to forgive her.

Forgive us our trespasses as we forgive those who trespass against us.

I'm not able to, not yet anyway. For twenty years I've blamed my mother for being narrow-minded and unforgiving. Now I recognise I'm my mother's daughter. Not narrow-minded maybe, but certainly unforgiving.

I have a sister. I imagine a conversation with Gee - another quest, someone else to search for.

The train slows up and then stops. I find myself watching a child run out into a back garden. The garden is bordered with a low hedge and is close enough to the track for me to see him racing after a ball. He may be three or four years old. He is wearing blue shorts and a tee-shirt with a cartoon character on it. As he runs towards the ball he trips and lays flat down on his tummy. The train windows are closed so I can't hear him cry, but I can imagine it well enough. Within seconds the back door to the terraced house opens and a woman comes out. She runs over to the boy and picks him up. She kneels on the grass and sits the boy beside her as she caresses his face and wipes away his tears. She starts to prod the child in the ribs and soon his face changes to a broad smile. She smiles too, she is tickling him and I can hear their laughter in my head.

Then the train starts to move again.

'You know what I'm going to say, don't you?'

I've told Gee about my sister and as usual she has listened attentively and remained expressionless.

'Probably,' I say.

'Enlist your mum's help. She's got another daughter out there somewhere and you've got a son. From the sounds of it your mother is pretty tough, she won't take no for an answer. Use that - maybe she'll get you the answers you can't.'

'But she doesn't want to find my sister.'

'She might say that, but I bet deep down she does. You can't have a child and not want to know what kind of life they've had. You know that well enough, Em.'

'Yes, well, I'm not my mother.'

'Mm,' is all she says, before she disappears into the kitchen.

Chapter 17
London

A couple of days after the harrowing trip to Hastings, Gee walks into the kitchen to find me bent over the sink.

'God, Em, you look dreadful. What did you eat last night?'

She rubs my back and then runs the cold tap, filling a glass with water. 'Here, sit down and sip this.'

As I sit, I pass her the sheet of paper I've been gripping in my hand. She reads it aloud.

To Emily Carpenter

You're looking for your son. I'm searching too, but my search is for my parents. It's a long story and a long shot, but I think we should meet. I'm in London, staying in the Southern Hostel next to Victoria Station. It will be easier if you can come here. Just write to me at this address with a day and time.

Patrick

'Oh, Em.'

She looks at me and then reads the letter again silently. She sits beside me and lays the letter down between us on the table and takes hold of my hand.

'Will you go? I mean he could be a nutter. The letter could be a hoax. You might get there and find no-one. How about we phone and try to speak to him first?'

'I will go,' I say, already rehearsing in my mind how it will be, what I will say, what he will say.

'Well, I'm coming with you then. There's no way you're doing this on your own.'

'Thanks,' I say and squeeze her hand tightly. Then in unison we both say, 'What about Ralph?'

At the sound of his name he looks up expectantly, having been lying at my feet pretending to sleep, but with one eye persistently looking out for any gift of a crumb that might fall from the table. Worrying about Ralph has helped defuse the tension. The letter sits between us, goading.

Roger is happy to have Ralph for the day, forgoing his usual Saturday afternoon fishing off the end of the pier.

'We'll be fine - boys together and we have no intention of telling you what we plan to get up to. Suffice it to say it will probably involve burger and chips and a pint or three.'

'Don't let Ralph have…' I start to say.

'I'm joking, Emily. Just relax, go off with your mate and have fun.'

'Yes, well,' is all Gee says. We haven't told Roger the reason for our London trip. We guess he will probably tell us we are mad to believe anything would come of it.

'He'll just say needle in a haystack or some such thing and then I told you so when we return empty-handed. Let's not give him the pleasure, eh?' Gee says as we make our plans.

I write to Patrick, offer him the date and ask him to ring Gee's number if he can't make it. When the day arrives and he hasn't rung, I can't decide if I'm relieved or disappointed, but more than anything I'm grateful Gee is there with me.

The night before the meeting I look through my wardrobe, discarding one outfit after another. Finally, I decide on a plain blue blouse and jeans. I spend ten minutes deciding between a linen jacket, a cardigan or a sweatshirt and finally choose a denim jacket. I look at myself in the mirror.

'You'll do,' Gee says, as I appear in the hall.

'Am I kidding myself?'

'Don't think too much. This is just a lad looking for his parents, chances are you will have nothing more in common than that you are both looking for someone. Let's go and enjoy the day and *che sara, sara* - as the song goes.'

'Yes, well…just as long as you don't sing it,' I say.

We are on the early morning train. Gee sits opposite me and we kick heels together, like a couple of kids.

'Are you okay?' she asks.

I shrug and then say, 'Do you remember pocket money?' I have a sudden memory of Saturday visits to Woolworth's, when dad would let me choose my own bag of pick and mix. I remember promising myself that one day when I had my own money I would spend it all on sweets, as many as I could possibly eat.

'We were too poor for pocket money,' Gee replies.

'Ah, you poor Irish waif.'

'What about pocket money anyway?'

'I was just remembering those pick and mix sweets, I haven't had any for years.'

'Here you are a wealthy author and you're craving sherbet dabs and liquorice. Excuse me, do you know my friend, the famous children's author? Ouch, what was that for?'

'Next time you'll have more than a kick. Keep your voice down.'

A few heads turn. A man looks up from his crossword, pen poised, raindrops of sweat on his forehead from concentration, embarrassment, or from having a body too large to fit into a single seat.

The train stops at Haywards Heath for more carriages to be added. Before I can stop her Gee stands up and shouts, 'All change please, all change'.

'What are you doing Gee, you crazy woman.'

'I've always wanted to do that. Ever since I saw it in an old black and white movie once. Who was it? Jimmy Stewart, or Trevor Howard, someone like that.'

A few people around us look flustered. I wish the seat would swallow me, or turn into one of Bond's ejector contraptions and catapult me into another universe. But instead I smile at an elderly couple who are holding hands and looking a little anxious.

'I apologise for my friend, she has a strange sense of humour. Don't worry, you don't have to get off, just relax and I'll try to get her to behave.'

The woman giggles quietly, while her husband puts their shopping bag back down on the floor, removes his jacket and puts it back up on the parcel shelf.

When the train arrives at Victoria the elderly woman stands and smiles at us.

'You can get off now dear,' she says, winking at Gee, before taking her husband's hand and stepping out onto the platform.

'Now that's what I call spirited,' says my friend. 'Remind me of that in forty years or so, will you?'

I'd suggested a midday meeting with Patrick and now I wish I'd made it earlier. With hours to spare I know it will only make the tension in my stomach a hundred times worse.

'Let's check out the exhibition in that new part of the Tate Gallery. Come on, we can pretend to be art critics.'

Two hours pass quicker than I expected and we focus our conversation on Turner's masterpieces and how we both prefer his work to Constable.

'I wish I was creative. Do you miss writing, Em?' she asks me as we leave the museum. 'I've never asked you. You did it for so many years. I used to think it was in your blood - that need to set pen to paper.'

'My head's too messed up. Sometimes I try to focus on a story, but if I give myself time to think I end up with the endless nightmare of this search that may now have finally come to an end. Do you think he'll like me? Or do you think he'll hate me for letting him go?'

'You're getting ahead of yourself. Remember, what will be will be. Let's not second guess. Let's just meet this guy and see what happens.'

She links her arm though mine as we head down into the Underground.

It's just before midday and we stand in front of the youth hostel, a featureless concrete building. I let Gee push open the glass swing door and follow behind her, like a defendant about to enter the dock. A girl is sitting at a counter that appears to be a reception desk of sorts. Gee steps forward.

'Hello, I hope you can help us. We've arranged to meet someone here, Patrick. He's one of your guests - we don't know his surname I'm afraid.'

Before the girl can reply, a young man comes out of the adjacent dining area and walks up to us.

'It's okay, Sandra, it's me they've come to see.'

We turn at the same moment to see a tall man, around twenty, with tanned and weathered skin and golden blonde hair. I search each inch of his face, looking for something, Johnny's eyes, his chin, anything that will connect me to this stranger. My mouth opens and closes again, without any words coming out.

'You're Australian,' Gee says. 'Sorry, I might be stating the obvious, but we weren't expecting... we thought you would be English.'

He gestures to us to follow him into the dining room, leaving behind a bewildered and fascinated Sandra.

'It's quiet at the moment, but it'll get busy soon for lunch,' he says. 'There's a bit of a garden out back, well more of a yard really, it'll be more private there to talk.'

We follow him down a corridor to a fire door that opens out onto an area of concrete, with several wooden benches and a picnic table. The table is littered with dirty glasses that I imagine have been left from the night before. We sit on one of the benches and he stands in front of us and then starts to pace up and down. I notice he is limping, dragging his right leg.

'Which one of you is Emily?'

'Me, I'm Emily,' I say.

'And I'm Geraldine,' Gee says. 'I think there's been a bit of a muddle. My friend here has been searching for her son and when we got your letter we thought...'

She doesn't finish her sentence because he holds up his hand. Then he puts his hand in his jeans pocket and pulls out his wallet. He takes a press cutting from it and unfolds it.

'This is you, right?' he says, pointing to me.

'The article is about me, yes.'

'And you're proud of what you've done?'

He glares at me, his eyes narrowing, but I can't see Johnny. I've thought about this moment hundreds of times. I was certain I would look at my child, all grown up, and know immediately.

'I'm not sure what you want me to say, or why you wanted to meet me. The child I'm looking for is English, he grew up in England.'

'Sure about that, are you?' His tone is accusing.

He opens his wallet again and this time he pulls out another press cutting. It's a small printed advert, the kind of thing you would see in a personal column.

'Know about this?' he thrusts the advert into my hand. I read it and pass it to Gee, both of us struggling to know how to respond to this angry stranger. The advert is from an Australian newspaper. It suggests there are people in Australia who may have undiscovered family in England. I look at Gee and she shakes her head. I hand the advert back to Patrick.

'I understand you might make a connection, but I'm sorry. I'm not the person you are looking for. My child was born in 1967 and he grew up here in England. I had to put him into care and the children's home found a family to adopt him.'

He stands and walks around the table turning away from us, dragging his right leg.

'So why not ask the children's home, they've got records, right? Why use the press to do your dirty work? My mother is out there somewhere, she could be someone like you, who thinks it's okay to abandon her child and then leave it twenty years before finding out anything about him.'

He pulls a chair over from another table, turns it around and sits astride it, leaning over the back of it with his chin on his arms.

'If the person who placed this advert is right, maybe that's what happened to me. I've come a long way and I'm not going back until I've got some answers.'

Chapter 18
London

For the next hour or so we listen as Patrick explains what brought him to England from the other side of the world. He tells us he'd been working on a cattle station in Queensland.

'I'm a good worker.'

He looks directly at us, challenging us to disagree. I guess he's had to fight his place in life many times.

'When they first see me dragging my right leg like it doesn't belong to me, I see the doubt every time. But once they see me on horseback, mustering and rounding-up, they know I'm good.'

'You live in the outback?'

I smile at Gee's use of a word we've both heard, without having an idea of what it might be like, in a country ten thousand miles from here.

'And you saw the advert?' I try to picture this young man, tired and dusty from rounding up cattle, coming across an advert that led him to travel across the world.

'It was the mention of England that caught my eye.'

As he pauses, I take a sip of water and study Patrick.

'Why would you think you were born in England?' I ask him.

'As far back as I can remember I've had a memory rolling around in my head. There's a man packing my case, telling me I won't need my jumpers. "*It'll be sunshine every day where you're going. You're a lucky boy. You're going on a big ship and when you get off you'll be on the other side of the world.*"

There is bitterness and sarcasm in his voice.

'Was it your father?'

He shakes his head. 'Sometimes I think it's a dream,' he continues. 'But it's always the same. I close my eyes and I can see the docks. People everywhere, some carrying their own luggage, others trailing behind a barrow carrying metal trunks, with a porter leading the way. There's a whole bunch of us kids. We walk up a long walkway, I can see the sea moving below me. I wonder what would happen if I fell in. I can't swim and don't like the idea of drowning in the cold, grey water.'

I'm caught up in the tale, but it's like hearing a story that's too far-fetched. Gee and I exchange a look and I wonder if she is thinking the same thing. And yet his tone is so measured.

'And you think because of that memory you might have been born in England and when you were little you went to Australia?'

As I wait for his response I realise it's weeks since I've had my dream about being in the clothes shop. Maybe my mind doesn't need to pretend anymore, now I have finally begun my search.

'I guess you think I'm crazy,' he says, with a glare that challenges us.

We look at him, but neither of us speak.

'There's so much I remember.'

'And your parents weren't travelling with you?' As Gee asks the question I can see she already knows the answer. 'You don't have parents, do you?'

'Everyone has parents,' Patrick says, 'but not everyone is lucky enough to know who they are.'

'No family? No brothers or sisters?'

'I remember an older boy being angry. He shouted at the man and I saw him crying when I left. I guess he was jealous.'

Gee and I are silent as we listen to this brave young man. As he speaks he gazes out of the window, as though his thoughts are still there, on the ship that took him from one world to another.

'There must have been a few hundred of us children. We were all told to stay together, don't run they said, you might fall overboard. The rest of the passengers, adults all wrapped up in smart coats and hats, they looked at us as though they had never seen children before.'

'It seems so impossible,' Gee says. 'Hundreds of children sent to Australia, without their parents? Why would such a thing have happened? It doesn't make any sense.'

His stands and glares at us accusingly. Then he dips his hand into the back pocket of his jeans and pulls out a tattered diary.

'It's all in there,' he says, handing it to me.

I hold the small diary in my hand and look at him. 'I don't feel comfortable looking inside, Patrick, these are your private thoughts.'

I think about my own diaries and how loath I would be for anyone to read them.

Gee looks from Patrick to me, then she stands. 'Why don't we take a walk together,' she says. 'We don't know London that well, but I'm sure we can find a park to stroll around.'

I hand the unopened diary back to Patrick, and Gee and I hover by the front door while he grabs a jacket, then the three of us walk side by side, occasionally having to change to single file as people bump into us.

'Arriving here in England must have been such a shock,' Gee says, after the third time someone knocks against her in their rush to get past.

'How do you people stand it?' Patrick says. 'The traffic, cars, motorbikes, buses, taxis, all weaving around each other. We've got space in the outback, so much space you can lose yourself and no-one worries you're lost.'

He falls back into step with us and I wonder if the walk is making his leg hurt.

'You're right, Brighton is the same,' I say. 'Everyone rushing, no time to look around them.' My thoughts go to Anglesey; I wish I was back there now, sitting beside Walter and gazing at the horizon.

It's easy to get lost here too, I think to myself.

'I never thought I'd feel lucky to have slept out under the stars,' Patrick says, 'but now I wonder what it would be like to have to jostle against people every day to go to work in a stuffy office. I might not have two good legs but I reckon if I'd been brought up in this country, my head wouldn't work so well.'

Gee touches my arm and points to a coffee bar across the street.

'How about we stop for coffee?' She goes inside the café, while Patrick and I wait outside. After a few minutes she emerges, carefully balancing three takeaway coffee cups on a little plastic tray.

'I don't mind you reading what I've written,' Patrick says, passing the diary back to me. 'It might help you to understand.' He stretches across and opens the book about mid-way through, pointing to one of the entries.

I read in silence, flicking slowly through a few of the pages. He has used the diary as a notebook, writing as though he is speaking aloud, giving himself a voice, despite having no-one to listen. He recounts some of his early childhood experiences when he first arrived in Australia. He writes about arriving at a children's home he refers to as *The Farm*. I don't need to read many of the entries to realise he endured years of cruelty at the hands of the people who should have been caring for him.

I stop reading, close the diary and hand it back to him. Gee is watching me and I wonder what she's thinking.

'You had no childhood, no love or affection,' I say, looking at Patrick, but thinking of Thomas.

By way of reply he hands the diary to Gee, she opens it and starts to read aloud.

'I was twelve when I found my voice and started to answer back,' she reads. *'Mostly I was sticking up for the little ones, the ones who used to cry themselves to sleep at night and who would get beaten in the morning for wetting the bed. There was one chap, his name was Forest. He walked around with a thick stick, always flexing it and threatening us with it. Anyway, I don't remember exactly what I said to him, but whatever it was he didn't like it. You could see he was pleased for the excuse to beat me. I made the mistake of looking up as he brought the stick down on me for the tenth time. I twisted around to look at his face and that's when I felt my leg give way. He didn't believe me when I said I couldn't stand. I laid on the ground for a while, then he made me crawl back to the house on my hands and knees. They wouldn't call a doctor, said I was making a fuss. They gave me a couple of weeks off from the labouring, but the leg was never properly reset. It eventually mended, but it's never been right.'*

'We can't imagine what your life has been like,' Gee says, her voice is a whisper. She flicks through a few more entries, but this time she reads in silence.

Patrick finishes his coffee, then stands and stretches.

'You're a brave young man,' Gee says, handing the diary back to him. 'You've come all this way on the strength of an advert and now you're sharing your private memories with a couple of strangers. But what makes you think Emily can help you?'

He is looking down at his hands. They are rough and callused, his nails short and cracked. He doesn't look up when he replies. 'I don't. Not really. That article I read about you looking for your boy, well, it got me thinking. But you haven't had much luck with your own search, so there's no point you helping me with mine.'

His answer is as sad as his story.

'We've both made a start, let's keep in touch.' I hold my hand out to him. 'Perhaps one of us will discover a nugget of information that may help unravel this tangled mess.'

Gee and I travel back to Brighton and spend a quiet evening, each absorbed in our own thoughts.

'I don't understand. Why were the children sent there in the first place?' Gee's angry voice breaks the silence. 'Someone must have allowed these children to be sent into the hands of these monsters. Then they just turned a blind eye once they got rid of the problem. Saving money, that's what this was all about.'

The next morning I wake early. I look out of the window and see white. Not mist, not drizzle, but oppressive air. It's as though the clouds surround me. They have come down to meet the earth. I open the window and notice the cloudy air has silenced all about me. It dulls the sound of the leaves rustling, even the traffic noise is muted. I try to imagine what it must have been like for Patrick, being transported from one world to another as a child. And now as an adult to return to his beginnings, only to discover nothing he recognises. He has no sense of roots or home. He is homeless in the true sense of the word.

Chapter 19
Brighton

My head is full of Patrick's words, his expression when he told us about his fears and sadness. Patrick is the same age as Thomas and when I close my eyes at night all I can see is that ship, full of little children, stolen from their homeland. A couple of days after our trip to London Gee is up early and out before breakfast. When she returns she slaps a newspaper down on the kitchen table.

'Look, Patrick didn't dream any of it, Em, this is worse than we can ever have imagined.'

The broadsheet has printed a double-page spread, exposing the horrors of an archaic system that started centuries earlier but had continued until the late 1960s. The article explains how a boat set sail from Southampton to Sydney, Australia with *'orphaned and abandoned children'.*

'But listen to this bit, Em.' Gee reads, *'No-one had asked them whether they wanted to go; they had simply been told they were going. They were wrenched from all that they knew, to be sent half a world away to fill the homes and orphanages of the British Commonwealth.'*

'Does it say there was more than one boatload then?'

'I can't bear to read it,' Gee says, slamming the paper down on the table.

I pick it and continue to read silently. The article explains that over many decades thousands of children were taken from their British homeland and sent to the colonies - Australia, Canada, New Zealand - to provide *'good white British stock'* to populate these countries. Many of the children were denied any basic education. They were told they had no family, that their parents were dead.

They were housed in institutions where the rules were harsh and there was no love or care.

'You're right about the money,' I say. 'This was a chance to save on child care costs and, at the same time, help out British colonies. It was a win-win situation. Except for the children. They had nothing to gain and everything to lose, their nationality, their family, their history.'

It has been several months since I started my search for Thomas and I've achieved nothing. Now I have to consider the impossible, my child might be thousands of miles away in another continent.

The last thing I feel ready for is a party, but Gee has been my saviour for so many years and Roger has been planning it for weeks. The party girl is about to be forty and this will be a party to surpass all parties, but Roger has sworn me to secrecy. Each time he catches me on my own he divulges another snippet. There's to be disco music and lights, plus a co-ordinated laser and firework show at midnight. The police and council have been informed.

'The thing is Em,' Roger sounds passionate even when whispering, 'it's not just her fortieth. It'll be twenty-two years since she joined *Black's*. She's our longest serving designer. I've tracked down loads of her past clients. We've got over a hundred acceptances already and there's still a fortnight to go. Can you imagine her face? Olly is planning to video the whole night. Phillipe is making a montage of some of her design work from over the years and we're making it into wallpaper to put up on the end wall of the office, it'll be there in perpetuity. Then there's the collage of photos. I'll admit I struggled a bit, we've got loads of her at presentations and client briefings, but none of her when she first joined.'

'When she was a scatty teenager with her head in the clouds and her eye on her next vodka?'

'Exactly. You must have a few shots of those wild years, the two of you getting drunk and ending up in the gutter.'

'I'm not sure she'll want to be reminded of all her past exploits, but I'll see what I can do.'

That evening I tip the contents of my holdall onto the bed and rifle through the bits and pieces. I know I have a strip of photos dating back to a few months after I'd arrived in Brighton. Gee and I squeezed into a photo booth in Woolworth's and pulled silly faces at the flashing light. She had offered to help me spend my wages on some new clothes.

'You can't keep borrowing mine,' she told me. 'Well, you can, but you need to find your own style. I think purple and black. It's perfect with your new chic blonde crop.'

We spent a glorious few hours in a boutique in the Lanes and I bought two outfits and wore one of them as we left the shop. A purple miniskirt, made to look like leather, but must have been some kind of PVC and a black ribbed polo sweater. Black tights and knee-length boots. I looked like a purple version of a zebra crossing.

Looking back at the strip of pictures I remember the way I felt. Excitement about my new clothes, the new me who had a friend to show me a new life. Free from rules and disapproving looks. At that moment, in that photo booth, I wasn't thinking about my son. I had discarded him and my life was moving on.

Roger's plan is for me to suggest a girls' night out with Gee on the Saturday before her birthday. I'm to tell her we have a table booked at Mario's, but on the way we will stop off at the office to tell Roger something. The story is that he's at work late planning an important pitch. It seems a bit convoluted, but he convinces me it'll work and that she won't guess. I cross my fingers behind my back when I tell her I've booked the table. A white lie my mother would say is still a lie.

Saturday arrives and I've booked us in for manicures in the afternoon.

'It's ages since we spoiled ourselves,' I tell her, feeling guilty at the thought of treats when I have so much to grieve for; my father, the sadness of Patrick's story. I wish I was from a country where the people wore black as an outward sign of grief. Meals out, parties, manicures are all too frivolous. I wonder what Walter would say.

That evening we get ready together, doing each other's hair, choosing jewellery. Gee is on form.

'This feels much more than a night out at Mario's,' she says.

I wonder if she has known all along and is playing the game so as not to spoil Roger's fun.

'Do you remember when we used to get ready for those nights out at *Leeroy's*? Lord, what a pair we were. Some days we'd start at four in the afternoon and we still weren't ready five hours later. Now we're all grown up and proper, or boring, depending on your point of view.'

'Trust me, Gee, you'll never be boring.'

'I'm in the mood for doing something wild tonight, just to remind myself what it's like to be young and carefree. I'll be forty next Thursday for heaven's sake, this might be my last chance. Going to join me?'

'Depends.'

'On what? Whether you get caught misbehaving? Don't worry, I'm not planning on breaking any Commandments.'

Whatever her plan is, I never find out. Instead, we stop at the office on the pretext of telling Roger he can join us at Mario's if he gets there by 9pm. After that, who knows where we might be. An unlikely ruse, particularly when Gee suggests we could just as easily have phoned.

'I'll stay in the car while you go in,' she announces, as we pull up in the office car park.

'He's your fella,' I say, pulling her out of the car and away from her favourite Beach Boys track.

This is only the second time I've entered the office building since I left *Black's* all those years ago. The décor is new; khaki, cream and fawn, running in horizontal bands around the walls. It's as though I am inside a chocolate bar.

Roger's office is on the fourth floor. Over the years *Black's* has expanded from niche designers to a multi-media agency, offering exhibition design, commercial photography and signwriting. *Black's* has reached a pinnacle of success, with a blue chip client base. Gee was in for a gold-plated party, with the boss pulling out all the stops.

We come out of the lift and head towards Roger's office, but the corridor lights are dimmed and there's no light on in his office.

'Oh Lord, he's not even here,' irritation is evident in her voice. 'He's probably disappeared to the pub. I told you we should have just phoned. We could be tucking into our olives and antipasti by now.'

'Stop moaning and let's check the boardroom, maybe he's in there,' I say, as I drag her with me down the corridor. I ignore her grumbling and pull her down towards the boardroom and push open the door. As it opens, the lights come on, music starts blasting and over a hundred people shout out 'Surprise'.

Gee is rarely lost for words, it's fascinating to watch her gaze around at the sea of faces, opening and closing her mouth like the proverbial goldfish. Roger is at her side, grinning. Finally she makes a sound, which is at best a squeal and at worst a shriek.

'You did all this.' She throws her arms around his neck and hugs him so tightly I worry he can't breathe.

'Pleased then?' he says, continuing to grin and then one by one all the guests come over and Roger is swept to one side as each person tries to monopolise the guest of honour. Instead, Roger makes his way over to me.

'Let's get you a drink. Well done for getting her here, it can't have been easy, I know how stubborn she can be. Likes her own way does Gee.'

'Thanks, large G and T please. Yes, she can be a tough one, but then we wouldn't want her any other way, would we?'

I stand to the side of the room, which is beautifully decked out with bunting, streamers and balloons, all colour co-ordinated with the floral displays on each table. I sip my drink and enjoy watching my friend's face as she spots people she hasn't seen for years, favourite clients, former work colleagues. I am entirely absorbed until someone taps me on the shoulder and makes me jump.

'I didn't mean to scare you, but it's Emily, isn't it? Terrence Fortune. Remember me? Your first boss and hopefully the best?'

Terrence shakes my hand energetically.

'It's great to see you. Do you know I never found a secretary as efficient as you.'

'My memory is that I was pretty rubbish to start with. You needed shares in *Tippex* with me around, for all the mistakes I made.'

'I've followed your career with interest. I always knew you would go onto great things. You were timid but there was a certainty about you, especially your writing. You were always picking me up on my grammar if I remember correctly.'

'What are you up to now, Terrence? Still in Brighton?'

'Yes, I left *Black's* soon after you in fact. Started up *Fortune's Publishing*. We specialise in non-fiction, otherwise I might try to poach you. We're always looking for new authors, if you're ever tempted to write your memoirs let me know. I hope your publisher...'

Terrence is interrupted by a commotion occurring on the other side of the room, which we can hear even over the music. Gee is standing in front of Roger and another man.

'Get out, just get out,' she shouts, over and over.

I can't believe any amount of alcohol would have suddenly transformed Gee from a happy, squealing birthday girl, into an angry harridan. I rush over to her and stand between her and the man she is confronting.

'Hey, calm down. What's up? This is your party, remember. You're the guest of honour and you're supposed to be having fun.'

'Get him out of here,' she shouts, pointing at the man who is standing beside Roger. Then she turns towards me, her voice almost loud enough to hear from the other side of the street, 'Did you know about this?'

'What? Know about what? Gee, whatever it is I think maybe you're over-reacting.'

I turn to face the man who is looking dismayed but stalwart. Roger is trying to pull him to one side, but he has no intention of leaving. Meanwhile a small crowd has gathered round, interested to see the spectacle play out.

'Come with me,' I take Gee's hand and pull her past the crowd and through the doors into the corridor. If the unwanted guest isn't going to leave the party, then it's safer for me to remove Gee. Once out in the corridor she pulls away from me and stands with her arms outstretched as if her whole body is vibrating with anger.

'How dare he. How did he even find him? Are you sure you didn't know about this?'

'Let's get a coffee.' She won't take my hand, but she does follow me down the six flights of stairs to the ground floor where the vending machine is helpfully sited next to several plastic chairs and a small coffee table.

Chapter 20
Brighton

'I'm guessing he's your brother?'

She looks at me, but the look in her eyes is cold. It's as if she is somewhere else, no longer sitting beside me.

'Come on, how about that coffee?' I say.

'Thanks, yes. Sorry.'

'What for?'

'For shouting at you. God, why did Roger have to meddle? Did you know what he was planning?'

'I knew he was planning a surprise party but he didn't exactly share the guest list with me. If I'd known, then I would have warned him off.'

We pull a couple of the chairs close together and sit beside each other. There is no-one else around and the darkness outside makes the fluorescent lights seem even brighter.

'We haven't talked about this for years, Gee. I remember the first time you told me.' I sip my coffee, my mind going back to the day a few months after I had shared my own story with Gee.

It was a Sunday morning and we had the house to ourselves. I was teasing her that we should be getting ready to go to Mass.

'Don't even joke about it. God and me, we fell out a while back and I'm not likely to be forgiving him any time soon,' she said, facing me with a serious expression that was so rare I barely recognised her.

'Well you know my thoughts on religion. It seems to me to be not much more than a way of controlling people. Or at least that was my mother's interpretation.'

'I haven't been completely straight with you, Emily, about my past. I didn't come to England to find work. I was running away.'

'From Ireland, or from your family?'

'Both.'

'I've always had an image of your family as being happy-go-lucky. Pretty much like you.'

'I'm a good actor.'

The cat that had welcomed me the day I arrived in Gee's house share wandered into the kitchen and sat between us on the kitchen table, occasionally turning its head from side to side, as though it was following our conversation. Gee told me that the cat appeared at the back door one day and decided to stay. They had never named it and now we all just referred to it as 'cat'. We weren't even sure if it was male or female.

'I have a brother,' Gee continued. 'His name is Gavin and his girlfriend was my best friend, that's how they met. In the school holidays she spent more time at our house than her own. She and Gavin were a great pair, full of mischief and fun.'

I stroke the cat and watch Gee fidget in her chair.

'Her name was Sinead.'

She is looking down at the floor now; she shakes her head as though the memories are so painful she can't bear to relive them.

'Sinead came to me one day and told me she was pregnant. She sat on the floor of my little bedroom and wept. I didn't know how to comfort her or what to say. We were just sixteen years old, for God's sake. We knew nothing. All I kept thinking was, it could have been me. She told me that Gavin knew about the baby and he'd told her to tell me and ask for my help. I didn't understand at first and then the realisation set in. I told

145

her I couldn't be part of it. We were Irish Catholic girls, through and through. Abortion isn't just against our beliefs and our families, it's illegal.

'I was so angry with Gavin, I was angry with Sinead too. I told her I couldn't help her. I said she needed to speak to her mother, get her to understand, to ask for advice.

'But the next day she came back, pleading with me. She'd found someone to do it. I told her Gavin must go with her, not me. She said he was scared. I shouted at her, then I remembered mum and dad might hear. I told her I'd think about it. Of course, I knew there was no choice. I couldn't let her go alone.

'I knew we couldn't delay, it would make it far worse. So the next day I met up with her, told her I'd go with her. But I made her swear never to tell my parents. I knew it would break their hearts. Not just the idea of the abortion, but killing their first grandchild. It was a dreadful time, Em.'

She pauses and takes hold of my hand. I see she is trembling.

'Gavin spent all the time avoiding me,' she continues. 'It was just as well as I couldn't bear to talk to him, to look at him even. The day I went with Sinead to that dirty room where her child was killed was the worst day of my life.'

She looks away from me, taking deep breaths. The cat has had enough fuss and jumps down from the table, but then decides to brush its tail against my leg as a reminder that it is almost time for food.

Gee continues. 'Afterwards, Sinead was very ill, she got a bad infection, nearly died. And then my thoughtless, selfish brother told my parents. When Sinead was so ill, he was frightened, went blubbing to our mother, told her everything. She blamed me, of course, her precious son couldn't possibly be at fault. She screamed and shouted at me, told me I was heartless, that I'd persuaded Sinead to commit the worst sin. It was murder, she said. She told me to get out of her sight, she never wanted to see me again. As far as I was concerned I was no child of hers.'

'Dear God. Honestly Gee, what faith tells someone to turn their back on their children - how can that be holy and good? Your mother, my mother, they are just a bunch of hypocrites.'

'Some people find it easier to follow rules.'

I think of my mother and realise that what I have thought of as stubborn strength is really weakness. It is easier not to question, not to try to understand, but to follow blindly.

Gee is staring at the floor, her breathing shallow and rapid. She doesn't look up when I speak, my voice almost a whisper. 'You must have been terrified when you first came to England, on your own in a strange country, no money, nowhere to live. No friendly Irish face to save you from yourself in a steamy café.'

'Well, as they say, what doesn't kill you makes you stronger.' She bends her head and I rub her back as she quietly sobs. I run through all the things I could say, but each sounds like a platitude. I say nothing and for a while we sit together in silence.

'It was the blackest time for me,' she says. 'Since then I've learned to live in the moment.'

'And all those dark thoughts?'

'They're vacuum packed, stored away, never to be reopened.'

I am brought back to the present by bright lights shining into the foyer of *Black's*. A car has pulled up outside. I watch as someone gets out and walks off, away from the building.

'Maybe it's time, Gee. Time for you to forgive.'

'I can't go back there, to Ireland, not now, not ever.'

I squeeze her hand tight, 'Your parents are older now, maybe wiser too about the way the world is. Isn't it worth a try? Speak to your brother, you've got a chance now he's here.'

She looks beyond me, her focus is out of the window where the street lights reflect back on the glass, creating patterns.

'Like I said, it's too late for me,' she says.

We sit for a while in silence; the coffee is cold but we sip it regardless.

'Are you ready to join the party again now?' I ask her. 'That's if everyone hasn't gone home in the interim. I haven't even tried the canapés yet and Roger has been raving about them for weeks.'

'Poor Roger, I was pretty awful to him, wasn't I? In truth there's no way he could have known about Gavin, about our history.'

'I'm pretty sure he thought it would be a good surprise.'

'Yeah, well...'

We use the lift to return to the fourth floor and hope to slip in unnoticed. The party is still buzzing and almost everyone is on the dance floor.

I take her hand and lead her into the room. 'It looks like the guest of honour wasn't too badly missed after all.'

Chapter 21
Anglesey

The events of the party have caused such tension between Gee and Roger that the atmosphere in the house is unbearable. I decide to return to Anglesey. It's the one place where I can think straight, decide on the next steps in my search. Plus it will be good to see Billy again and I'll be making one dog very happy into the bargain. I tell Gee my plan. She doesn't say much and I get the sense she is a little embarrassed.

'Have a good time and when you get back I will hopefully have myself together again.'

'Don't be too hard on Roger.'

'I'd put it all behind me, or thought I had. It was a shock seeing Gavin again.'

'Well, remember that Roger only wanted to give you the best birthday surprise. Cut him some slack.'

'Surprise, yes, I think we can safely say he achieved that. Safe journey and come here when you get back. Try to persuade that Walter fella to come with you, I'm dying to meet him – tell him we have some pretty good park benches in Brighton too. '

The morning I leave a letter arrives. The response to Jocelyn's article has tailed right off, so I am not expecting this to offer any significant help. I stop at a service station mid-way on the journey and enjoy a coffee while I read the letter, which is from Patrick.

Dear Emily, he writes.

I promised I'd let you know if I found out any more about my past. I reckon there's someone who might help you find Thomas. It's a long shot, but anything is worth a try.

There's a girl here at the hostel, her name's Anna. She's been helping me, coming along to a couple of meetings I've had with a woman called Marjorie. It turns out Marjorie is the woman who put the advert in The Melbourne Daily, the advert that made me come to England.

Anna and I went to see her and showed her my birth certificate. She said lots of the children who were sent overseas had their names changed, even their birth dates. So there's no saying that Patrick is even my real name. It's all such a jumble in my head, but Anna keeps telling me to stay on course, I've got nothing to lose, I've come all this way after all.

I'm going to see Marjorie again in a few days' time, so I'll write and let you know how I get on. I'll ask her if she can maybe help you find Thomas.

Cheers

Patrick

Perhaps he's right, maybe something connects Patrick's search with mine, but it's as though I've dropped a precious jewel into sinking sand, the more I try to grasp it the more it falls away.

I'm making no plans on this trip to Anglesey and don't know how long I'll stay, so we drive straight to *Four Elms* guest house, hoping Ralph's garden room is waiting for us.

Catherine comes to the door with hands covered in flour and some interesting smudges of chocolate splashed across her apron.

'Hello again. It's Ralph and Emily, isn't it? You're just in time for chocolate brownies. Come on in. In fact, the oven timer is pinging, 'scuse me a second.'

Catherine's relaxed welcome is what I need. She puts us in the same room as before and Ralph disappears straight out into the garden.

'There's a get-together in the village hall tonight, if you fancy it. You'll see some familiar faces I'm sure. But you've had a long drive, maybe you just want to put your feet up.'

It's late afternoon and although I know exactly where Ralph is hoping to go, we just have a brief stroll around the park and then it's a hot bath for me and bed.

I haven't told Gwen we were coming, so when I knock on her door late the next morning, the look of delight on her face is as good as a hug.

'Oh, Miss Emily. Oh my, Billy will be so thrilled to see you, but he's at school until this afternoon. Can you come back? He'll be mortified if he knows you've been here and he's missed you.'

I laugh and taking her hand, I step into the hallway. Her home feels comfortably familiar.

'How about I come with you this afternoon, to meet him from school?'

'Of course, he'll be jumping for joy. Then he'll want to show you off to all his friends. The minute he found out you are *the* Emily Carpenter he's told everyone in the village. Said how he's had lessons from a famous author. And now we're working our way through your books. We get them from the library and we're on number three at the moment. Even the librarian has to hear all about it every time we go in. *I know Emily Carpenter, she's given me tuition,* he tells her. Good job the librarian likes children.'

'That's brilliant, Gwen, I'm so pleased for you both.'

'Oh, you should hear him with his words. It's tuition for him, not plain old lessons. His reading and writing have come on no end and it's all down to you.'

'You and Billy should take most of the credit, all I did was point him in the right direction.'

Catching up with Gwen and Billy was fun, but tracking Walter down might not be so easy. On Friday morning we get up late; the Anglesey air casting a relaxing spell on me.

As soon as breakfast is over and I put on my walking boots, Ralph is poised and ready. As we head towards the cliff-top I try not to look too far ahead. Autumn has arrived and with it a healthy covering of crumpled leaves are scattered on the ground. The summer has been drier than most which, according to the weathermen, means we are in for a colourful autumn. The leaves still on the trees are turning to copper, auburn and gold. A gust of wind shakes the branches and the leaves fall ahead of us, as if a royal carpet is being laid out.

I can understand why Walter has chosen this place. The quiet villages, the huge stretches of farmland and empty beaches mean that people can go about their lives at a gentle pace. The folk I've met have time for each other, with a chat at the supermarket check-out, or a shared joke when standing at the post office counter. Brighton might offer theatre, clubs and bright lights, but the trade-off is traffic and queues and too many people. It's ironic that I feel lonelier in those crowds than I do here in this small community. I wonder what Gee would think of this sleepy village. I guess she would hate it.

I am deep in thought, so when I hear birdsong I look down to check Ralph is still beside me and just catch a glimpse of his tail as he dashes across to Walter. He sits at Walter's feet and gazes up adoringly.

'Hello,' he says, as I approach.

'Hello.'

'We were just passing,' I say, smiling.

'Yes, I see,' he says and pats the space beside him, beckoning me to sit down.

'I owe you an apology.'

'Do you?'

'I was rude to you the last time we spoke. I'd like to blame it on a hangover, but I'm not sure that had much to do with it.'

'Maybe stick to lemonade?'

I look up at him and see he is smiling. 'Ralph been behaving?'

'He's missed these walks.'

'Me too,' he says.

'Are you busy with the harvest, or is it too early?'

'There's a lot to do on the farm, before the weather turns. The autumn will be beautiful this year, but the wind will come too soon. We won't be able to enjoy these colours for long. We need to enjoy what we can when we can.'

I've met Walter just a handful of times and yet it feels so easy to talk to him, as if the words are just waiting to tumble out of my mouth.

'My father died.'

He holds his hand out, letting me put my hand in his.

'I'm really sorry to hear that. It must be a difficult time for your mother.'

'I thought he would always be there.'

He nods. 'Fathers can be like the rock you cling to in the rapids. But that rock can also weigh you down when you are trying to swim.'

'Did you know your father?'

'He was a bricklayer. He got contract work, worked on some big building sites. Back-breaking work. He'd be off to work before I was up most mornings. On site by 7am, even on the dark winter days.'

'And were the two of you close?'

'People travel to London to find their fortune. I had to leave to find mine.'

'Would you ever go back?'

He shrugs and looks towards the horizon. 'I had a blinkered view of life when I lived down south. Too many obstacles obscuring my view.'

'You're right. So much of life is about smoke and mirrors, isn't it?'

He studies my face, then smiles.

'My children's books keep selling, but it all seems so false. I don't deserve the success.'

My focus is on the pile of leaves that have gathered under the bench.

'Success gives you a voice. You could use it for good.'

He stands and beckons to me to follow him. Ralph trots behind us, sniffing the leaves.

'I've met a young man, his name is Patrick. His story is so sad, Walter.'

Patrick's story has been rolling around my mind since the day I met him. It still seems so dreadful I can barely voice it now.

'Children were taken from England and sent to Australia and treated in a terrible way.'

'Australia?'

'They were used as child labour, beaten and worse. So much has been hidden for so long.'

He doesn't speak for a few moments and when we reach another bench he sits.

'The thing is, this young man, Patrick…'

He turns towards me, waiting for me to continue. 'He is looking for his parents. The reason he contacted me is because…'

'You're looking too?'

'I had a child.'

'When you were young?'

'Too young. Although I didn't think so at the time.'

'What happened.'

'My mother made me give the child away and I've been so angry with her for so long. I can't get beyond it. I've finally been brave enough to ask questions and I'm sure she knows more than she's saying, but I can't get a straight answer from her.'

'I know about anger,' he says. 'It can really mess with your head.'

He takes an apple from his pocket and using his penknife he cuts a piece off and gives it to Ralph.

'Let's walk together,' he says. 'Ralph is getting restless.'

We walk for a while longer and I watch Walter throw sticks for Ralph.

'Answers aren't always what we need,' he says as he picks up another stick. 'Sometimes we need to stop asking questions.'

Chapter 22
Anglesey

That evening I sit in the armchair and Ralph leans his head on my foot. Catherine has lent me some CDs and I choose some relaxing Mendelssohn to soothe me while I try to digest Walter's words. Maybe I need to forget about my search for Thomas. I've left it too many years and based on the accounts that Patrick has shared with us, then Thomas might even be in another continent.

The next day is wet, so we choose to stick to the pavements for our walk, much to Ralph's dismay. But after that comes one of those rare autumn days when the sky is Wedgewood blue and the sun casts shadows in every direction. After breakfast we sit out in the back garden of the guest house. Ralph finds the perfect spot with his head in the shade, and the warmth of the sun on his back.

'What would you like to do today?' I ask him, 'or is that a silly question? Okay, it's up to the cliff-top, but first let's take a trip into town. I need to visit the bookshop.'

Bookshop visited and a surprise parcel tucked away in my bag for Billy, we stroll up to the headland. I buy a sandwich and an apple from *Brian's Bakery* and as I leave I have second thoughts and pop back in for another, just in case.

Sure enough Walter does not disappoint us and as we approach he waves. It's only then I realise perhaps he is as keen to see us as we are to see him.

'Cheese and pickle, or cheese and salad, your choice,' I say, opening up the paper bag and offering it to him. At the sound of the paper rustling, Ralph sits alert, with his gaze fixed on the sandwich wrapping.

'Er, no, sorry old boy. But you can have some apple if you're patient.'

'Let's share, one of each,' Walter says, as he takes one half out of its wrapping. 'Thanks, much appreciated.'

He takes a bite and then says, 'Do you miss the bright lights of the city?'

'Living in the south is pretty confining. There are so many people and they all want a piece of you.'

He nods and says nothing for a few moments, as though he is considering something.

'We never really own anything in this life and yet the idea of ownership has led to many crimes.'

I'm not sure what point he is making.

'Are you thinking about the children who were sent to Australia?' I ask him.

'Adults, children, they can all be treated like possessions. Men used to believe they owned their wives, objects they could pick up and put down at will. Serfs were made to work the land by wealthy landowners. If we allow ourselves to be owned we forfeit the right to choose. Slavery comes in many forms.'

'These children were taken from their homeland, some of them were treated worse than animals. If you heard Patrick speak about what he went through it would make you weep. No-one knew, or at least those who did turned a blind eye.'

He finishes his sandwich, screws up the wrapping and walks over to a nearby rubbish bin, which is close to overflowing.

'Has Patrick managed to find out about his family? Does he know why he was sent away?'

I shake my head. 'He let us read his diary, much of it is a jumble of memories. He's just desperate for answers. The newspapers have been printing articles about it, they are referring to them as the child migrants. It seems to me that children were treated like commodities to be traded between countries. Shouldn't we be learning more about how to treat people with each generation? Seems we know less now than they did in the Dark Ages.'

Ralph looks pleadingly at the apple that sits on the bench between us.

'Children should be loved, cherished, cared for,' I say, bending to pat Ralph on the head.

'You're right and it makes me angry too. But I've spent so long trying to shake off that anger I don't want to think about the terrible things people do to each other, in the name of religion, or politics. And you know, it's not just children who need cherishing, it's adults too.'

'You mean my mother, don't you? You think I'm being harsh. I should forgive. But I can't forget. I'm not like you, I can't let go of the anger.'

'We can only change the things we're responsible for.'

'We're back to ownership again, aren't we?'

'Pretty much.'

Ralph has his share of the apple and we walk together to the cliffs, looking down at the shingle beach. The tide is out and the sun throws a shimmering light onto the rock pools.

'Same time tomorrow?' I say, holding out my hand to shake his.

When I ring Gee to touch base she tells me she has received a note from Patrick, asking me to ring him at the hostel. I try twice before I manage to speak to him. He tells me he has been out sightseeing with Anna.

'She sounds lovely,' I tell him, forming a picture of her in my mind.

'It's down to her I've found out more about my past,' he says.

He goes on to explain that Anna went with him on another visit to see Marjorie, the woman who placed the Australian advert that started off his search.

'Marjorie asked me if there was anything else I could remember from when I was little.'

I listen while Patrick tells me about the mouth organ he's had since he arrived in Australia.

'I can't remember a time when I didn't have it. When I gave it to Marjorie she looked at it, real close, turning it over in her hands. Then she asks me about my name. My birth certificate says Fitzpatrick Lloyd, but I dropped the Fitz because I was always getting teased by the other boys. What kind of name is that to give a lad?'

Before he continues I start to guess where his story is leading.

'It seems the people at *The Farm* would have used my surname, that's what they did back then. So Fitzpatrick is my surname. I don't know, to be honest, it's all a right muddle.'

'And did she think that would help? Now she knows your real name?'

'She says they have all sorts of names in their files, folk looking for children, and grown-up children like me, looking for answers. She's going to see if there's a Fitzpatrick among them and if there is, well, we'll take it from there.'

'That's wonderful, Patrick. I'm so pleased for you. You've done so well and it's great you have your friend, Anna, there beside you.'

'There's something else.'

I fish for more coins from my purse and slot them into the phone box, waiting for him to continue.

'My mouth organ.'

'The one you've had since you were tiny?'

'Yep, well, there's two scratches on one side. At least I've always thought they were scratches. But Marjorie points at them and tells me, *Look, here's your initials, LF, Lloyd Fitzpatrick.*'

I feel a chill run through me, which I know has nothing to do with the weather.

'So, you have a memento from your past, something to link then and now. Marjorie sounds like a wonderful person.'

'I don't feel that lucky right now,' he says, 'seems like I don't even know my own name.'

I promise to stay in touch and ring off.

Reflecting on Patrick's story leaves me feeling unsettled. Later that afternoon Ralph and I wander up to the cliff-top. I'm just approaching Walter's bench when I hear his whistle and there he is, standing beside me.

'Good morning, you look deep in thought,' he says, as he stretches his hand down to stroke Ralph.

'It's been an interesting day.'

'Good interesting?'

'The lad I told you about, who is searching for his family. We've kept in touch and now it seems he's getting closer to answers.'

'That's good then,' he says and sits down beside me.

While Ralph snuffles among the grass and leaves beside the bench, I tell Walter about my conversation with Patrick. When I reach the part about the initials on the mouth organ, he puts his hand up, signalling for me to stop speaking.

'His name is Lloyd Fitzpatrick,' he says.

'Yes.' I study his face, trying to second guess the next thing he is about to say.

'Walter, what is it?'

'I knew we had met for a reason,' he says, his eyes glistening with tears. 'That's the way of nature, it pieces things together that human beings try to tear apart.'

'I love your riddles, but this time I'd rather you unravel your words for me. What is it? Can you tell me?'

'Let's walk and talk, or at least I'll talk and this time it won't be in riddles.'

Chapter 23
Anglesey

'My mother sewed,' Walter says, smiling at the memory. 'She did alterations for people, made curtains. All work she could do from home. She'd make our tea, put me to bed, then sit up until the small hours with her sewing machine. She worked every day, no days off, no holidays, and just earned pennies. She took great pride in her work. People used to say her hand-stitching was neater than any machine could do.'

I have an instant image in my mind of his mother, a short lady, her hair neatly pinned up in a bun, an apron permanently wrapped around her middle, glasses propped on the end of her nose, and delicate fingers working magic.

'We didn't have a lot at home,' he continues, 'but what we had we shared. Food was basic, but there was always enough bread and jam to fill me up if I was hungry. Mum and dad rented a little terraced place. Damp in the bedrooms, outside privy. Neighbours who looked out for each other. Then when I was ten everything changed.

'Mum fell pregnant. I didn't understand much of it, but I could tell they were worried. I thought they were worried about money, that there wouldn't be enough to feed another mouth. But later I found out it was much more than that. It seems that when she gave birth to me the doctors warned her not to get pregnant again. She had a weakness and in the end giving birth a second time meant the baby lived but mum lost her fight. I came home from school that day and dad just said, *"Your mum's not coming home, Walter."* And that was it.'

He is quiet for a moment before continuing.

'I didn't know about my brother until later. It was a couple of weeks on and dad came into my room. I remember it was a Saturday. *"We need to pack a case for you, Walter,"* he said. *"Make sure you put all your favourite things in and your bird books, don't forget those."*

'It was dad who taught me to watch the birds. Not far from our house was a river, and on a Sunday morning we'd sit on the riverbank and he'd test me. *"See that one, diving in, picking up a fish." "That's easy, dad, that's a kingfisher,"* I'd tell him.

'He taught me to listen to their song, practise whistling it. His whistling was so clear that if I closed my eyes I wouldn't know if it was dad or the bird. And he bought me two bird books with beautiful coloured drawings of each bird and all you needed to know, their nesting habits, what they ate, which ones migrated in the winter. I read every page, learned about all of them, so I knew I could always give him an answer when he tested me on those Sundays.'

'Is that when you started to draw?'

He nods. 'I copied the drawings in the books. I was rubbish at first, but gradually I got better. Dad said I had a real flair for it.'

I study his face, grip the edges of the bench and wait for him to continue.

'I asked dad where we were going. I thought maybe it was going to be our first holiday. Just dad and me. But it wasn't a holiday. Turned out we were too much for him, my brother and me. There was no way he could go to work and care for a little baby and he didn't think it was right to separate us.'

Part of me wants to stop him now. I don't think I can bear to hear the rest of it, to watch him reliving the pain of that time.

'I've often wondered why he didn't just find a new home for my brother and let me stay. But then I figured he'd promised mum. And someone had to look out for the little one. Someone who was family. That was my job and I failed miserably at it.'

'Whatever happened wasn't your fault, Walter, you were a child.'

'We got a bus,' he is looking away from me as he speaks. 'Dad didn't say much on the journey and when we arrived at *Wrattan House* I got to meet my brother for the first time. *"Here's your baby brother, Walter,"* he said. *"It's your job to look after him now. You're grown up and he's just little."*

'And then he put a small box in my hand. I knew it was his mouth organ. He told me to give it to my brother when he was old enough to understand. Dad had always played the mouth organ, as far back as I can remember. *"Make sure you teach him to whistle those bird songs,"* he told me. *"Then, the music and the whistling, that's what will always connect the three of us."*

'My dad left me there in *Wrattan House* and I watched him walk down the path with his shoulders hunched, like he was carrying a load of bricks on his back. He didn't turn around. I didn't see my dad again.'

'He never visited?'

He shakes his head.

'Mr and Mrs Collins ran the home. Whenever I asked them they said dad was busy working and he'd entrusted me and my brother to their care.'

'What were they like?'

'Mr Collins wouldn't stand any cheek and his way of keeping control was to use his belt. We all had the belt on a regular basis, even though I don't think we were bad kids. Mrs Collins tried to mother us, but she was a timid little thing. Whenever her husband was around she did what he told her. He didn't believe in mothering, said it would make us too soft.'

'But you were just children, you needed love.'

'When we first arrived my brother was the only baby there. There were twelve kids altogether. He was the youngest and the eldest was fifteen. There were only two girls, twins they were, pretty little things, long blonde hair. All of us boys used to try to get in their good books, doing their chores for them in return for a peck on the cheek.'

'Did you help to look after your brother?'

'Mrs Collins took a real shine to the baby. Treated him like her own. But once he was about two years old and in his own bed, he was moved into my room. That's when I'd tell him things. I told him about our mum, how hard she'd worked and how clever she was at sewing. Told him all about dad, what he looked like and about the bricklaying. And I told him all about the birds, showed him my books and got him to learn the names. I suppose it was me who taught him to read, by pointing out the letters and saying the bird names over and over.'

'The two of you must have formed a special bond.'

He shook his head, as if trying to shake away some of the memories.

'There were a lot of dark days, but sometimes in the school holidays we'd have a day off from our chores and Mrs Collins would take us all to the woods. She let us run around, climb trees, kick a ball. She'd keep hold of my brother's hand all the time, wouldn't let him out of her sight. I'd sit with the two of them and it was then I'd point out the birds.

'*Look Lloyd,* I'd say, *remember that one? It's a chaffinch. Listen to its song. Isn't it pretty?*

'Anyways, it seems that Mr Collins was having none of it. He didn't like us having fun. It was when we came back from one of our woodland trips that I heard him shouting at her. *He's not yours, he'll never be yours, face it woman.*'

'And that was the reason for it, I guess. Some time later Mr Collins came into our bedroom. He told me to pack a bag for Lloyd.

'*Where he's going, Mr Collins? I asked him. What about my case Mr Collins? I need to go with him 'cos I'm his big brother and it's my job to look after him.*'

'But he told me to shut up and pack the bag. He said he was a lucky boy, he'd been chosen for a great adventure, off on a big ship to a country where the sun shines every day.

'Lloyd didn't want to go on any ship. I shouted at Mr Collins, beat him with my fists, but he just pushed me away. I didn't want Lloyd to be scared, but I couldn't help myself. I cried and cried when they took him away, made myself sick with it.'

He has his hands covering his face now and I can barely hear his voice. The silence is broken by birdsong, but I don't know enough to recognise which bird is singing. Walter would know, but right now he is in such a dark place even birdsong isn't helping.

'You must remember every moment of that day,' I say, laying my hand gently on his shoulder.

'He was five when they took him. The two girl twins went as well. Just the three of them. Packed off never to be seen again and there was no sign of Mrs Collins that day. I reckon he locked her up somewhere so she couldn't stop Lloyd being taken.

'Every day after that I asked Mr Collins if I could write to Lloyd. But he told me to forget him. *He's off to a better life now*, he said. Then a few weeks later Mrs Collins walked out the front door with a small case in her hand and never came back. The authorities came round, said Mr Collins couldn't run the place on his own, so we all had to be moved on to other homes. But I was almost fifteen by then and told them I could manage alright on my own. I said if they put me in another home I'd run away every day. I reckon they thought it was easier to just let me go.'

I imagine Walter as a young boy, wandering the streets of London alone.

'Where did you go?'

'First off I thought I'd try to find my dad. I had an idea that with his help I could find out where they'd sent Lloyd, maybe get him back so we could all be a family again. I went to the house where we'd been living. I knocked on the door and a woman answered. She said she didn't know anything about a Mr Fitzpatrick. She told me to get lost and not to come back.

'I went to all the building sites around the docks, asked if anyone knew him, if they'd seen him about. I just drew a blank. It'd been nearly five years since I'd seen him and for all I knew he could be dead. Eventually, I decided it was about time I looked out for myself for a change.

'All I could feel was anger. Anger at Mr Collins for stealing my brother and at Mrs Collins for giving up on us. Mostly though I was angry at my dad for letting us go, for not coming to visit and for not keeping in touch.'

'It must have been impossible for your dad. He must have believed he was doing the right thing for you both.'

As I say this I remember what Walter has said to me about my mother, about forgiveness.

'There's something I don't understand. If you told Lloyd that his mother had died, how is it that he's come all this way to try and find her?'

'I didn't.'

I look at him and for a moment I'm tempted to hug him to try to take away his pain.

'I lied to him,' he continues, 'I couldn't tell him the truth, that she died bringing him into the world.'

'What did you tell him?'

'Just that mum and dad loved us, but couldn't cope, that there wasn't enough money for food. It was a truth of sorts.'

'And your years at *Wrattan House*?'

'They called it a children's home, but I knew that if that was a home I didn't want a home ever again.'

'Is that why you came here to Anglesey, to live on the land?'

'I chose live-in jobs at first, errand boy in small hotels, where they'd give you bed and board. As I got older I worked in a few cafés and the like, where they had a spare room over the shop. I lived on chips for years.

'But all the time I'd think about Lloyd. I'd wonder where he was, whether I'd ever see him again. On the odd day off I'd find a river or a park with a lake. I'd just sit there, watching for birds. I'd whistle their tune, like dad had taught me and they'd whistle right back to me.

'After a few years I knew I needed to find somewhere I could breathe. It took me a while to find this place, but it's the closest I've ever been to feeling at home.

'But before Lloyd left I gave him dad's mouth organ. I managed to put it in his case when Mr Collins wasn't watching. I whispered to him that it was a gift from dad, that when he was old enough he should open it up and learn to play.'

I take a deep breath and hold out my hand to him.

Chapter 24
Anglesey

It looks as though Gee might have her wish after all. Walter is thinking of coming south with me, at least as far as London. But before we can make plans, straight after breakfast the next day, Catherine calls me into her lounge. The anxiety shows on her face.

We stand together and watch scenes of devastation flash up on the television news. The south coast has experienced winds of eighty miles an hour, wreaking havoc, with properties destroyed and lives lost. A tear-stained face appears on the screen, a woman reporting that she woke to find her conservatory had disappeared, lifted by the winds and transported to a neighbouring property. I watch incredulous as the journalist explains that twenty-three lives have been lost. Six of the seven oaks, that gave the Kentish town its name, have fallen. People are trapped in villages, place names I know well, just a stone's throw from my childhood home.

'Those poor people,' Catherine says, as we continue to watch the film footage. 'We've been so lucky here. It must have been so frightening.'

I think of my mother alone in her house.

'I should ring my mother, just to check, you see…'

There is too much to explain.

'You must use our phone, it's a dreadful day out there and the last thing you want to be doing is standing around in a telephone box. I'm just going to sort the kitchen out. I've not cleaned up after breakfast yet.'

'Thank you,' I say, as she disappears into the kitchen.

As I dial the number I imagine my mother walking to the phone and her surprise to hear my voice. The phone rings. I wait. I let it ring and ring. There is no response. I picture her lying outside in the back garden, hit by a falling roof slate. I wonder how long she's been there, who will find her.

Catherine comes back into the lounge. 'Did you reach your mother? Is everything okay?'

'She's not answering,' I say, not wanting to accept I may have made the wrong decision.

'Perhaps the line is down. They said on the news that a lot of people have lost power, I'm sure telephone lines are down as well. Why not try again in a little while?'

This morning's walk is sombre. Ralph trots steadily beside me and we circle the park. No sticks are thrown and no squirrels are chased. The trees dip and sway in the strong gusts of wind and I try to imagine the scenes in my home town, with branches strewn across roads and normal life shattered by the forces of nature.

Before returning to *Four Elms* I decide to try once more, from the phone box at the end of the road. Mum picks up on the first ring.

'Emily, are you alright?'

'I'm ringing to ask you the same thing, mum. The winds, I saw it on the news. Has there been much damage at home?'

'Jennifer, next door. She thought it best to move her car in the middle of the night when things were really bad and she got a terrible fright. The noise, Emily, it was as if the world was ending.'

'Was Jennifer hurt?'

'No, nothing like that, but she moved her car out of the way of a tree and then the roof of the garage next door to her came right off. The car is completely squashed. Thank the Lord she wasn't in it at the time.'

'But you're okay?'

'Yes, yes, I'm fine. All the pots in the back garden are smashed and one of the fence panels has broken. You know, the fence your dad put up all those years ago, it's lasted well enough I suppose.'

'Do you have any help mum? Is there a neighbour who can give you a hand?'

'Oh, I'm fine. I'm going next door in a minute to help Jennifer. There's the insurance to contact. You only just caught me. I've popped in to get some milk. Are you in Brighton? They say it's been bad all along the south coast. Is Ralph okay?'

'I'm not in Brighton mum and yes I'm fine. We're fine.'

'Good, that's good. Emily, when you left…'

'Let's not talk about it now, mum. You go back to Jennifer, she'll be worrying. I'll ring again soon. Good luck with the clearing up.'

It's time to go home. There are fences to be mended and it's not just those damaged by the wind. I make one more visit to see Billy before leaving. Gwen has asked me to stay for supper and tells me Billy has a surprise for me. This time I buy a cake and remember to take it. As I hand it over to Gwen she smiles.

'Thanks, Miss Emily, carrot cake is Billy's favourite. He's just washing his hands. The table's all laid. Come on in and take a seat. How about a glass of wine to celebrate? Like I said, Billy has a surprise for you.'

A few minutes later the door opens and Billy bursts in, his face flushed with excitement.

'Miss Emily, Ralph. We're so pleased you could come. Aren't we, mum? Has mum told you yet? She said I could tell you. You haven't told her yet mum, have you?'

Gwen smiles and shakes her head.

'I promised Billy. It's your news, so you should be the one to tell her.'

'Well, the thing is, I wrote a story,' Billy stands on one leg, barely able to contain his enthusiasm.

'That's great Billy, well done. What was the story about?'

'No, miss, that's not all of it. I wrote a story for a competition and I won. First prize. Look miss, I won a certificate and everything.' Until now he had his hands behind his back and now he holds out the certificate for me to read.

'Billy, congratulations, that's great news. *In the Anglesey Primary School story competition First prize is awarded to Billy Jones.* You must have written a wonderful story. I hope you're going to frame that certificate, Billy, put it up in your bedroom as a daily reminder that you are a writer.'

'I'm a writer? Do you hear that mum? Miss Emily says I'm a writer.'

'I do Billy and she's right. You are a clever boy. Just think how far you've come since we first met Miss Emily.'

'The thing is Billy, I started just like you.'

'You did?'

'Yes, I won a competition at school and instead of a certificate I won a big tin of chocolates.'

'Oh, Miss, maybe chocolates would have been a better prize?'

'No, you can't hang chocolates on a wall, can you? But the important thing is that you're a writer now. It doesn't matter what you've won, and you need to keep on writing. I didn't know about your good news, but I have a gift for you and I reckon this is the perfect gift for a writer.'

I hand Billy the parcel and watch him carefully unwrap it.

'You're very kind, Miss Emily,' Gwen says, 'you shouldn't be buying presents for us. What do you say, Billy?'

The boy's face tells me all I need to know. As he handles each book and opens the covers his expression is one of pure wonderment.

'Oh miss,' is all he says and then he takes one of the books over to his mother. Gwen reads out the inscription I have written on each of the title pages.

To Billy, from your friend Emily.'

'You have the whole series there Billy, all the books I've written. And one day maybe you'll be able to give me one of your books, a book you've written.'

'I will miss, yes, I will. And I'll write in it, *To Miss Emily, from your friend Billy.'*

Chapter 25
London

'Are you happy in the front beside me?' I ask Walter, as he stands beside the car, looking doubtful. His rucksack is laden and instead of throwing it over his shoulder, he is holding it in front of him, supporting it with both arms, as though it is a child.

Ralph looks up at him, as if he is waiting for one nod from his friend to confirm he can ride all the way on Walter's lap.

'I haven't left Anglesey in a long while,' he says.

I wasn't able to give Walter much time to think about this trip to London but, as ever, he was philosophical when he had just one day's notice to get packed.

'I've waited many years to see my little brother, I don't want to wait anymore,' he says.

But now, faced with the reality of the journey back down south, with all its memories, I can see he is apprehensive.

'I'll be fine,' he says, 'he's travelled thousands of miles. A short ride in a car is nothing. Let's get going, shall we?'

'I wonder if your brother has your talent for drawing?' I say as we head off.

'There will be a lifetime to learn about. I doubt he'll remember me, he was so young when we were separated.'

When I think of these two brothers meeting again after so many years I want to jump and sing with joy. I whisper a *Thank you* to the Universe, or Fate, or whatever it is that has meant this gentle man is at last able to be reunited with the brother he had promised to look after.

I asked Walter if he wanted to speak to Patrick on the phone. It didn't feel appropriate for me to be the one to break the news. Walter suggested I ring the hostel and leave a message. Wording the message wasn't easy. In the end I just said, 'Can you let Patrick Lloyd know that Emily Carpenter will be visiting him tomorrow and that she will be bringing along someone who really wants to meet him.' I hoped that would be enough to keep him around and about the hostel for our arrival, but not so much as to make him anxious.

During the journey down to London we have the chance to chat, but there are long periods of silence too. I get the sense Walter is preparing what to say to Patrick, but maybe also remembering how things were for them the last time they were together. Patrick was five years old and Walter a young teenager, both of them abandoned by a father who felt he had no choice.

'Life is strange,' he says, as we pull off the motorway to have a break.

'I'd agree with you there.'

'I wasn't searching and yet I've found my brother, but your journey is ongoing. I'm sure you just haven't found the right path yet. Don't give up.'

After Walter told me about his past, I shared my own story with him. He said very little, but when I reached the part about my decision to leave home when I was sixteen, he smiled and said, 'Seems we are both runaways.'

Now in the motorway service station, I feel infused with fresh hope that I'll be as lucky as Patrick and Walter. 'I have no intention of giving up. I'm angry with myself that I've left it so long, but I'm inspired by this. You and Patrick, finding each other. It makes me believe in goodness again, I'd lost that for a while.'

'Life is like a bicycle wheel, it will continue to turn even if some of the spokes are missing, but when they are all in place the wheel is stronger. Lloyd and I have done okay up to now, we've managed, but…'

'But now you've found each other your lives will be richer?'

'Like I say, the wheel will keep turning.'

I smile. I love Walter's riddles and I wonder what Patrick will make of his big brother.

'Will you call him Lloyd or Patrick?'

Walter doesn't answer, but quietly sips his coffee.

'This place is good preparation for the city,' I say, looking around the restaurant. 'If you think this is busy you wait until we reach London. The contrast with the peace and beauty of Anglesey couldn't be starker.'

'We can swap birds and sheep for people,' he says.

'I'm not sure I'm with you?'

'In the countryside I watch the animals, try to learn from them. Here I can watch people, imagine what's brought them here, where they may be going next. I can guess at how they're feeling, what their hopes and dreams are. Everyone has hopes and dreams, even people in a service station.'

'You are lovely,' I say, immediately wishing the words had stayed in my head and not appeared out of my mouth. 'Sorry, I didn't mean...'

'It's okay, so are you,' he says.

We return to the car and give Ralph a quick stroll around the car park. My face still feels flushed as we prepare to drive off. To cover my embarrassment I turn on the radio.

'How about some music, just classical maybe?'

'Music is fine, any type, I don't mind and don't be embarrassed. We're friends and friends can say anything to each other.'

For the last part of the journey we talk about the music and the traffic, which builds up all around us as we approach London.

'I can hang around for a while, go and sit in a café or something, or we can go in together,' I say, as we pull up near to the hostel.

'Fate brought you to me and had a hand in Lloyd meeting you. I think fate has chosen you to be a part of the reunion.'

As we approach the hostel I'm as nervous as I was the first time I met Patrick, but then I had Gee to calm me down. This time I'm just a bystander, but that doesn't stop my stomach from fluttering as though I haven't eaten in days. When I go up to the reception desk and ask if Patrick Lloyd is around, I'm surprised the receptionist can hear me over the thunderous noise my heart is making in my chest.

Walter seems calm, but I imagine his exterior does not reflect the turmoil of emotion he must be feeling inside. He has spent years developing his serene approach to life, but I am sure this scenario will be really putting it to the test.

Patrick comes out from the games room with a girl beside him. I look over his shoulder and see several lads standing around a billiard table, chatting. He walks towards us, looking at me and smiling.

'Hello, it's good to see you, Emily. I got your message. I'd like you to meet Anna.'

He sounds proud as he introduces a waif-like girl. Her hair is tightly braided and curled around her head like a turban. She has so many freckles on her face it's difficult to see space between them.

'Anna, this is Emily Carpenter.'

Neither of them seem to have noticed Walter, who is standing patiently beside me.

'Emily Carpenter,' Anna says. She is flushed and beaming. 'The Emily Carpenter. Patrick told me about you, but still, to meet you in person. I've read all your books, some of them I almost know by heart, well bits, you know, phrases.'

It's a while since I've come face to face with any of my readers. I do a quick calculation and think she must have been a late starter, or perhaps her reading habits haven't changed since she became a young woman.

'You're thinking I'm too old to be reading *Peter and Polly and the Lost Treasure* and all the rest of them. But that's where you're wrong. There are messages in your stories, grown-ups should read them too, they'd maybe learn a thing or two.'

I smile and shake her hand. Her innocence and openness are a joy. I'm pleased that Patrick has Anna in his life.

'It's lovely to meet you, Anna. Patrick, I have someone for you to meet too. This is Walter. Walter, Patrick.' This feels so inappropriate. I am introducing brothers to each other as though they are acquaintances at a party.

'Hi Walter,' Patrick says, holding out his hand.

Walter shakes his hand, but keeps hold of it for a few moments more and I can see that Patrick looks uncomfortable. Anna slips her arm into Patrick's, watching his expression.

'Shall we go and sit somewhere quiet, where we can talk?' I say, turning towards a corner of the entrance area where there are a few bookshelves and several armchairs grouped around a coffee table. We all sit, but no-one speaks.

Then Walter says, 'We've travelled from Anglesey, but I understand you've travelled all the way from Australia.'

'Yes,' Patrick says, relaxing a little as he speaks. 'I've come to England to try to find my family. It's a long story...' The expression on Patrick's face changes. He looks at me and then back at Walter. Anna shuffles in her seat, as though she senses this is the culmination of Patrick's long journey.

'A story with some of the chapters missing,' Walter says, gently. 'Maybe I can fill in some of them for you. Let's take a look at that mouth organ of yours. It's many years since I packed it into my brother's case before he went off to Australia.'

'Your brother?'

'Yes.' Walter takes Patrick's hand in his and holds it and this time Patrick does not pull away. The two of them look at each other without speaking and I turn away as the tears run down my face. I will remember this always.

Anna stands with me and we head towards the door. I explain that I need to move the car before I get a parking ticket. I don't think the brothers even hear me.

Chapter 26
Hastings

Arriving back in Hastings is an anti-climax. The intensity of emotion I felt as I watched the reunion of the two brothers makes me miss Thomas even more. I want what they now have, but part of me feels as though they deserve it more than I do.

I go back to Tina Caraway's guest house and am relieved she has a room free. She even offers to look after Ralph for a while and tells me not to rush back.

When my mother opens the door I see her glance down and spot a fleeting look of disappointment on her face, before she looks up at me and smiles.

'No Ralph? Is he well?'

'Hello mum. I left Ralph with a friend. I thought it would be easier on Sparky. At least she won't have to hide in the bedroom.'

'Oh, Sparky isn't with me anymore. She was old of course, but I do miss her. It seems each time you come I've bad news to give you.'

We walk through to the sitting room and I notice part of the hem on her skirt is drooping, with a thread dangling across her stockings. As she turns towards me I see her blouse is spotted with grease. Wisps of her hair fall against her face. I look down at her feet and notice her slippers don't match.

'Shall I put the kettle on, mum?'

'Yes please. Do you mind? I haven't got myself together yet this morning.'

I look through the cupboards for biscuits. There were always biscuits in the house, but then I remember she bought them for dad. I notice several tins of cat food sitting on the worktop. I wonder if she has put them there to throw out, or whether she has simply forgotten they are there. The furniture in the sitting room is in exactly the same place as my last visit. Dad's empty chair still faces the television and his spectacles sit looking lonely on the nearby coffee table.

'How are you, mum?'

'Oh, I'm fine, thank you. How are you?'

We are like strangers still, but then I have spent more years living apart from this woman than with her. Walter's words tumble around in my head. *Parents are just people and people make mistakes.* We don't have anything to share except the difficulties that lie between us. It's a wide river with no footbridge. I'm sad that she remains on one side while I'm on the other.

'Who helped with the fence panel, mum? I see it's all fixed. And what about Jennifer next door, are the insurance people being helpful?'

'Not really. There are so many claims, it'll take time is all they'll say. But she comes with me on the bus to do her shopping. Not that I need much.'

Her voice drifts off and she looks lost in thought.

We pass some time drinking tea, discussing trivia and then she says, 'We waited many years to have another child. To have you. There was a time when we thought it wasn't to be. We'd had our chance. But then, when I was thirty-six I found I was pregnant.'

Patterns repeating. I haven't told her about my miscarriage, my second chance at motherhood. She shifts in her seat, preparing to speak again.

'You were a gift we didn't expect. A gift from God. We believed he was saying he forgave us.'

I want to shake her. I have allowed her entrenched beliefs of sin and punishment, confession and forgiveness to seep into my soul. I've fought against it for years and yet my thoughts follow the same tramlines.

'And that's why I did it. Do you understand, Emily?'

I see a woman who has never looked outside her beliefs, never questioned. Not for the first time I wish dad was here. I want to hear his slant on this story that has formed the bedrock of my life.

'No mum, I don't.'

'God had forgiven us you see. I didn't think we'd be as fortunate the second time around.'

I think about the catechism I'd learned as a child. For a child to be taught about sin, hellfire and damnation is the worst kind of horror story. My mother will have had the same black thoughts implanted in her as a child. She has lived her life in fear. She couldn't keep her sin a secret from the one being she really cared about - her God. The all-seeing, all-knowing spirit who judges all actions, words and thoughts.

But Gee is right, endless regret, anger and recriminations just keeps me in the past. Walter said the same thing. There needs to be a way to reach acceptance of what's gone and then, perhaps, the avenues open up for hope. Right now that feels like a long way off.

I watch her as she puts her cup and saucer down.

'There's something else I need to tell you, Emily.'

She stands and walks across to dad's chair. She puts her hand on the back of the chair as though she's hoping for the strength he might have given her. I'd always thought she was the strong one but now, seeing her drift into old age, I'm not so sure.

'What is it, mum? Is it about Thomas?'

'Thomas? Yes, I remember now that was the name you chose for him. We told the children's home, you know. We said, *his name is Thomas.*'

'Thank you, mum, that means a lot.'

She continues as though I haven't spoken. 'Your dad and I never used that name, it made him too real. If we did talk about him, which wasn't often, we called him the little one. But each year on his birthday your dad would raise the subject. *Have we done the right thing, Flo?* he'd ask me. Never expecting me to answer. And then on the baby's fifth birthday he begged me. *Let's go to the home. Just to see if he's alright, to make sure he's happy. We don't even know what he looks like. Do you think he's got Emily's eyes?* Your dad loved your pretty face you know. He was never prouder than when he pushed you out in the pram when you were such a little thing. People would stop to look at you and he'd say, *She's got big wide eyes, chocolate brown they are.* I'm sure sometimes he'd poke you to wake you up just to look at those eyes.'

She pauses and from the expression on her face I can see she's drifted off to a time when I was just a baby.

'You were saying, mum, about Thomas's fifth birthday.'

'Yes, that's it. Well, your dad kept on and on at me, so we got the train to Brighton. We put on our best things and I made sandwiches. We tried to treat it like a regular day out, but deep down we knew it wouldn't be a happy day. We caught the bus from the station, the number 51, and got off near to *St Joseph's*. It was a short walk, but I remember it was pouring with rain and windy too. Dad had brought a brolly, but he made me hold it and wouldn't think of sharing it with me. *I've got my cap Flo, I'm alright.* Do you remember that cap, Emily? He always wore it on days out. I've still got it in his wardrobe upstairs.'

I could see my father carrying the bag with their packed lunch, rain dripping off his cap as mum walked steadily beside him, struggling to keep the umbrella from turning inside out.

'Did you see Thomas, mum? What happened when you arrived?'

I'd promised myself I wouldn't ask questions. Walter had said that questions don't always lead to the answers you want, but I couldn't help myself.

'*St Joseph's* is run by nuns, you know. At least it was then.'

'I know, mum, I've been there. Remember, I told you when I came last time. I went there and they were singularly unhelpful, they wouldn't tell me a thing. They said all their records had been burned in a fire.'

'A fire? Well I don't know about that, but that day we saw a nun. Sister Perpetua her name was. Tall, graceful, angelic face. I told her we'd come to see our grandson.'

It's the first time I've heard her use that word and it suddenly makes my loss more tangible.

'I told her it was his fifth birthday and that we had bought him a present,' she continues. 'Could we just see him for a few minutes, I said. Dad didn't say anything, except to apologise for the rain that was running off his cap and coat. And then the nun told us, she couldn't help us. *When the babies are handed over they advise families it's best to let go completely, maintaining contact is not a good idea*, she said. Who for? I asked her. Not a good idea for who? Then she went on to say that most of the children were found new homes, new families, and contact from their birth parents or grandparents would only distress them. We could rest assured he was well and happy. Then she thanked us for coming and showed us the door.'

The same phrases repeated over fifteen years.

She pauses again as if she is reliving the ignominy of that moment.

'She wouldn't even let us leave the present.'

She turns away from me and goes out into the hallway and I'm left standing, still looking at dad's chair. I follow her upstairs. I think she's going to her bedroom. I wonder what has changed since dad died. Does she still sleep on the same side of the bed? How often does she put her arm out to find an empty space beside her? Instead she stops outside the door to my old bedroom. The room I sat in when Thomas was growing inside me. The one I returned to when I was alone again. I had always imagined that as soon as I left home she would have removed any evidence of me, given the room a fresh start. Instead, as she turns the wooden knob and pushes open the door I see a shrine. I gasp and it's only then she realises I am behind her.

My teenage bedroom is unchanged. The orange candlewick bedspread still covers the bed. The orange alarm clock they gave me for my fourteenth birthday shows 9am. My popstar posters still cover the walls. The only thing that has changed in my sanctuary of twenty years ago is the position of the armchair. The mottled brown chair with worn arms that used to be beside my bed, well placed for me to throw my clothes onto each night, is now beside the window.

Mum watches me as I walk around the room, touching each piece of furniture, reminding myself of the days and nights I'd spent in this room, thinking of the person I was then.

'I come in here often,' she says. 'Every day now your dad's gone,' she looks at me as though expecting me to question or criticise. I say nothing.

'I talk to you, tell you about my day. I've done it for years, ever since you left.' Her voice is matter of fact. 'It was all I could do. You'd left, I had no address, I couldn't write. I needed to tell you things. Your dad didn't like it, he said it wasn't healthy.'

'Oh mum,' I walk over to her, put my hand on her shoulder and ease her down to sit on the edge of the bed and I sit beside her. She looks away from me out of the window at the garden and beyond. Then she gets up and walks over to the chest of drawers. She opens the top one and takes out a parcel. The wrapping paper is intact. Tiny blue trains run across red tracks, criss-crossing this way and that, like snakes and ladders.

'We kept it you see. Put it away in your room, it felt like the right place. It's a wooden railway engine. Your dad chose it, the wheels turn and there's even a little driver who sits in the front cab.'

As I take the parcel from her I see she's crying. The tears run down beside her nose and she doesn't move to wipe them away. It's as if she doesn't even know they're there.

'Mum,' I say, 'don't cry, I'm here now.'

Chapter 27
Brighton

Overnight I have an idea and concoct a plan. In the morning I ring Gee and run it past her, certain she'll agree. After breakfast I drive round to mum's to find her still in her dressing gown.

'You're coming on a trip with me,' I tell her. 'Let's find your best frock and help me pack a small case. I'm not going to take no for an answer.' She follows my lead and appears happy to relinquish control.

I look through her wardrobe and find a smart claret dress and a silver grey cardigan. She says very little, but looks mystified when I take a small suitcase down from the top of the wardrobe and brush the thick layer of dust from it. I wonder how many years it's been since she last used it.

'Let's pack enough for a few days for now. Mum, you do your undies and personal bits and I'll sort out skirts and tops and shoes.'

A couple of hours later and we're ready. I leave a note for the milkman and partly draw the curtains. The fridge is virtually empty and the little that's there I deposit in the bin.

Throughout the journey she looks out of the car window, like a child going on their first adventure. She clutches her handbag tightly on her lap and shakes her head when I ask her if she wants to stop en route for a drink.

I'm reminded of days out with both of them. If we went anywhere it was always by train. Dad would bring a crossword book and when we weren't looking out of the window watching spring lambs, or freshly harvested fields, he would challenge me with clues, pretending he didn't know the answers. Mum would give us reprimanding looks if our voices got too loud.

Gee welcomes us at the door of number thirty-six. That evening her carefree chatter makes for a comfortable supper time. Roger has opted for a pie and pint at his local to keep out of our way and to make matters less daunting for mum, for which I'm grateful.

After supper mum offers to help with the washing up and Gee waves her away.

'Just sit and relax Mrs C. Chat to Ralph, he's taken a shine to you alright.'

My mother has said little since she arrived. It's as if she feels she needs to mind her manners. There's a stiffness about her and I realise that she may never have stayed in someone else's house before.

'She's lovely, Em,' Gee says, as she hands me a drying up towel, 'with all you've told me about her over the years I was expecting an ogre. But she's just a little old lady. A sad little old lady.'

'Losing my dad has changed her. It's as though she's lost her drive. No-one to boss around anymore. Even her cat died.'

We wait until the morning and then over breakfast we tell mum our plan. Seeing mum here in Brighton I start to think it might not be a good idea, but Gee is insistent. Mum doesn't agree or disagree and then as we get ready to leave she puts a hand on my arm.

'Wait a minute, Emily, there's something I need to get from my room.'

She comes downstairs with her coat and a shopping bag and we set off. We catch the No 51 bus and then walk a few minutes to South Street. I form a picture in my mind of that day fifteen years ago when mum and dad took the same walk. A day of wind and rain. Today, by contrast, it is crisp and clear. The early morning frost still dusts the shaded parts of the grass verges.

Gee has rung ahead and made an appointment for a Mrs Carpenter. She was vague about the reason for our visit, and when the nun opens the front door to us she looks perturbed.

'Mrs Carpenter?' she says, looking at each of us in turn.

It's at this point that my mother finds her voice for the first time since she arrived in Brighton.

'I'm Mrs Carpenter and this is my daughter, Miss Emily Carpenter and her very good friend Geraldine O'Connell. May we come in?' Then, without waiting for a reply, she steps into the hallway, past the nun who looks more than disenchanted with her impolite guests.

'You'd better come in here, Sister Angelica will be with you in a moment, she's just finishing morning prayers.'

My mother nods and then sits down at the side of the large mahogany dining table that fills the centre of the room. She gestures to Gee and I to sit either side of her.

'Can I get you anything while you wait?' the nun asks.

'Tea would be nice, thank you,' my mother announces. I know Gee is craving a coffee, but this is not the moment to mention it.

A few minutes later a tray of tea arrives, followed shortly afterwards by Sister Angelica, who sweeps in slightly breathless, as though she's been running.

'I'm sorry to have kept you, it's a busy day, we have had a celebration for one of our older sisters. Now, how can I help you? Mrs Carpenter?' I catch her eye and see a flicker of recognition, but then her eyes settle on my mother.

'Shall I pour?' I say, as much to ease the tension as anything.

'Yes dear, pour your tea and then perhaps Mrs Carpenter can explain how I can help. I'm not too sure of the reason for your visit. I apologise for not being better prepared, but Sister Patricia is never very good at taking messages.'

'My grandson,' mum says. My son, her grandson. He was here in this building, maybe even in this room we're sitting in.

'Your grandson? I'm afraid you'll have to help me with a little more information.'

'My grandson was brought here as a baby and we'd like to know what happened to him. His name is Thomas. Emily is his mother and she has a right to know.' My mother fixes her gaze on Sister Angelica and her tone is defiant.

'Ah yes, I thought I recognised your daughter. You came here a while back Miss Carpenter, that's right isn't it? We did explain to you then, I'm sure. We took in many children back in the sixties and seventies. But now children are placed directly with foster families wherever possible and then adopted. We are more of a closed order nowadays. We spend much of our time praying and helping the poor. As for your grandson, Mrs Carpenter, I'm afraid that what we told your daughter on her previous visit still stands. All our records were burned in a fire and as a result we have no information about where the children went to when they left here. But rest assured they would have been placed with a good, loving Christian family.'

'I don't believe you,' my mother says. She glares at the nun with a defiance I remember from my childhood. Gee looks at me and raises an eyebrow. I put a hand gently on my mother's arm, but she shakes me away.

'Mrs Carpenter,' the nun says, 'I don't think it's wise to make a scene.'

'I don't believe the records were burned in a fire. I think you're lying to us.'

Here is my mother, Catholicism ingrained deep within her, accusing a nun of lying. I feel as though I'm dreaming.

'You would have had to notify the authorities if you placed a child somewhere. Are you telling me all their records were burned as well? Do you know what today is? It's my grandson's birthday. He will be twenty today.'

'I'm sure he's had a good life, Mrs Carpenter. Enjoyed many happy birthdays.'

'Not if you sent him away he wouldn't have. If you sent him to Australia to be a slave.'

The night before we left Hastings, I sat beside my mum's bed and told her about Patrick, about the children who were transported and then abandoned. She was so quiet that I didn't think she had believed a word I was saying. Yet now I realise that she had absorbed every syllable.

'Mrs Carpenter, I'm not sure where you've got that idea from, but I must ask you to keep your voice down please. Several of our sisters are elderly and they may be taking a nap. Your shouting may alarm them.'

None of us have drunk a drop of tea and I can sense Gee fidgeting on her chair. We are getting nowhere and all we are achieving is raising my mother's blood pressure.

'Mum, it's time we went. Come on, let's go home.' I pick up her bags from the floor and pass them to her and as I hand them over I see coloured wrapping paper peeping out from the top of the shopping bag. My mother has brought Thomas's birthday present with her.

Gee opens the door and we file out, with Sister Angelica following behind us. As we walk towards the front door I look to my left and see that a door to a nearby room is partly open. I look into the room and see a nun sitting in a wing-backed armchair. She is wearing a nun's habit, but no head covering. Instead, on top of her head, is a coloured party hat. I drop behind the others and push the door open further to see a line of birthday cards on the mantelpiece. The number 80 appears on several, and there are the remains of a birthday cake on a small coffee table beside the window.

'Hello,' I say to the nun, who is looking at me with interest. 'Many happy returns.'

'Thank you. Would you like some cake?'

By now Gee and mum are standing behind me. Sister Angelica pushes in front of us, keen to interrupt the conversation.

'There's no time for cake now, I'm afraid, Sister Luke. These ladies are just leaving,' she says, as she moves to close the door.

'Would you like to read my cards?' Sister Luke's voice is hopeful. 'I've had one from Father Joseph. He never forgets. He's met the Pope you know. I was given a chance to meet the Pope, but I couldn't leave my duties here. I was responsible, you see, for the children.'

'Sister Luke is tired now, she's had a busy morning. If you'd like to follow me, I'll show you out,' says an increasingly anxious Sister Angelica.

At this point my mother moves forward, pulls up a chair beside Sister Luke and sits down.

'It's my grandson's birthday today,' she says.

'The children have all gone now. We'd line them up when families came. They'd pick the prettiest and the quietest. Mind your ps and qs we'd tell them or you'll get left behind. No-one wants a noisy child.'

'That's enough now, Sister Luke, it's time for your nap,' Sister Angelica says, trying again to usher us out of the room.

But now my mother is engrossed. She takes Sister Luke's hand.

'Do you remember my grandson? It's his birthday today too.'

For a few moments the elderly nun does not reply, as if she is searching through her memories. Then she says, 'He was noisy alright, but I always had a soft spot for him. He had the same birthday as me you know. Yes, that's it, it's his birthday today.'

I hold my breath as my mother remains calm and continues.

'What happened to that little boy, Sister Luke? Do you remember?'

By now there is little that Sister Angelica can do but fume silently as she loses control of her interfering guests.

'We got him all ready. We told him, *You're off on a great adventure to another country far, far away, where there'll be blue skies and sunshine every day.* I packed a cake for him too, for his birthday. He would have been five years old during that boat trip.'

We walk in silence to the bus stop. Gee holds my mother's arm and I walk along beside her. We have come so far and yet it's as though we have only just reached the starting line.

By the time we are back at Gee's house mum looks pale.

'Go and have a lie down, mum. Do you want a cup of tea to take upstairs?'

She shakes her head and heads up to her room. Gee and I sit at the kitchen table.

'Your mum was awesome, Em, incredibly brave.'

'Strong willed. I fought against it for years and now it's the part of her I need the most.'

'You're on the same side you know. I think you always have been. Flo and I had a heart to heart last night.'

'You and mum?'

'Yes, you were sleeping soundly and I couldn't, so I came down to find her chatting to Ralph, well giving him some digestives actually. She told me about the day she got that first letter from you, the one you sent from Anglesey.

'I remember the rage I felt when I got her reply. I don't think it would have made much difference what she wrote in that letter. But I'm beginning to understand how hard it's been for her.'

Gee nods, then moves over to the sink to fill the kettle.

'Your mum said how dreadful it was that first time you went to see her, the day she had to give you the bad news about your dad.'

'What did she say?'

'She said she opened the door and saw you standing there and she didn't see the confident, successful and well-respected author. She saw her little girl, the quiet child who suddenly found her voice when she reached thirteen, when you started asking questions and never stopped.'

'Yes, I remember being a bit of a pain with all the questions.'

'Apparently you were always asking her things like, *Why do you believe in God, mum? Where we do go when we die, mum? What does our soul look like?* She said she always sent you to your dad and she had no idea what he used to tell you, but whatever it was it kept you happy for a while, until the next subject cropped up.'

'I sound pretty annoying, don't I?'

'Your mum thinks you're a lot like her, you know. She said she recognised a spark that might have led her to quite a different life if she'd ever given it a chance.'

'Did she talk about my dad?'

'She did, but it was so sad to see her little face. It just crumpled up whenever she mentioned his name. She said how thrilled he would have been to know that you'd come back. She told me he would have held your hand and quietly listened to your questions, always knowing the right thing to say.'

The kettle is boiling, but neither of us want a drink. Gee turns off the gas, sits beside me and holds my hand, as I lay my head on the table and weep.

Chapter 28
Anglesey

I have come so far with my journey, which looks to be pointing me in a direction I never guessed I would take. Before making any more decisions I need to visit Marjorie. She did so much to help Patrick piece together his past, maybe she can help me too.

This time I make the trip to London on my own, leaving mum with Gee and leaving them both in charge of Ralph. Or perhaps it will be the other way round.

I'd formed a mental image of Marjorie from Patrick's description. Her curly brown hair and grey-blue eyes matches my image of her. Her expression when she gestures to me to sit reminds me of a gentle shepherdess guiding her sheep to safe pastures. But as I look around her office and see the piles of files and notebooks covering every available inch of desk and floor, I realise she has taken on a task that could last her a lifetime. I gaze around at the papers, guessing that within each one is the story of a life, with so many unanswered questions.

'Can you help me to find my son?' I ask her.

She smiles, moving her hand across the desk, moving some of the papers to one side.

'What can you tell me about him?'

I tell her what little I know, his age, his name. I tell her about *St Joseph's* and about the nun who remembered giving him a birthday cake for his journey to the other side of the world. She listens and makes notes.

'You understand that it is difficult to find out much from here. We need to discover if he did go to Australia. Some children were sent to Canada, or New Zealand.'

As she speaks the impossibility of it makes me feel dizzy. Each time there are pauses in our conversation I think of Walter's advice; it's not all about questions and answers and yet…

'Why was it allowed to happen?' I ask her. 'Shouldn't someone be held to account?'

'I can't think about that now. All my focus is on helping people find their loved ones, it's about trying to give them a future, when many of them are trying to forget their past. I'm planning another trip to Australia. It's the only way to hear their stories first hand.'

I know what she is suggesting without her saying the words.

'You think I should go too, don't you? To make my own search for Thomas.'

'It may be the only way you will discover what happened with any certainty.'

I think about the flight and then I think about the journey that Thomas must have made.

'He wasn't even five years old,' I say, biting my bottom lip hard, to try to remain in control of emotions that are threatening to overwhelm me.

'If you can go, it might give you some peace,' she says.

'He might not even be in Australia.'

'That's right, he might not.'

Back in Brighton that evening I tell Gee and mum about my meeting with Marjorie.

'Will you go to Australia?' mum asks me.

'You're not going on your own,' Gee's voice is defiant.

'It won't be cheap,' mum says.

'Roger will help, he owes me a bonus anyway,' Gee smiles.

Mum lays a hand on my arm. 'Emily, I don't think I can manage such a long journey, but I've got a little pot of money put by. I want you to have it. It's not much, but it might help if you need to travel around. Australia is such a big country.'

'Mum, that's really kind, but it's fine. I have enough and we can live cheaply, stay in hostels.' I pause and they look at me expectantly. 'But first we need to go to Anglesey, together.'

Patrick wrote to me soon after his meeting with Walter.

Dear Emily

Thank you seems like a pretty ordinary way to explain how grateful I am for what you have done for me. I don't think I ever really believed I would find my family. I still feel like the whole thing is a bit of a dream and one day I will wake up and I'll be back in Oz and alone again.

Walter has asked me to go up to Anglesey with him. The way he describes it sounds more like the kind of place I will feel at home and if I'm with him then it will be the first time in my life I'll know what it's like to live in a family.

You remember Anna? You met her at the hostel. Well, Anna is coming along with us. She says she doesn't have anything better to do, but that's Anna's way of saying she really likes the idea.

Walter says it will be easy for me to get work as there are so many sheep and I can try my hand at shearing, which is something I always fancied. I watched enough of it in Australia and in the spring we'll help with lambing. Anna's going to get work too, she can turn her hand to most things. So between us we should be able to get enough money together to rent a little place. My brother says it will feel strange to have a permanent roof over his head, but then right now everything seems pretty strange - even writing 'my brother'.

We're not going to try to find our dad - for now at least. Too many years have passed. Walter says there's no point in looking back anymore, now we all have a chance of a future we could never have dreamed of.

It would be good to see you again if you are ever up this way. I guess you are still searching for your son. You are a good person and you deserve some luck.

Cheers
Patrick

This third trip to Anglesey is like a homecoming. Mum sits in the back seat with Ralph, who lays his head on her lap for most of the journey. Gee has left a freezer full of meals for Roger and made him promise not to spend every night in the pub.

I phoned ahead and booked *Martha's Cottage*. It will give us a chance to spread out and means we could cook for ourselves rather than eating out every night.

'Ever practical Emily,' Gee teased when I made a list of provisions we could take with us.

Mum insisted on making sandwiches for the journey. She'd been acquiescent when I'd suggested the trip, intrigued almost. 'I've heard these motorway stop-offs are overpriced. You don't need to waste your money.'

Gee's suitcase is crammed full of jumpers, hats and gloves.

'We're not going to the North Pole, you know, it's only North Wales.'

'It's not the south coast though, is it? Everyone knows it always rains in Wales. Does this cottage of yours have central heating?'

It's late afternoon by the time we arrive. Martha has left the key under the front door mat. The log fire is lit and she's left a small hamper of fruit and vegetables on the kitchen worktop.

'Oh my,' mum says, as she takes in the charm of the place.

Gee opens the fridge door and calls out in delight, 'Now this Martha is a girl after my own heart. Not only has she left us milk, butter and cheese, but there's an acceptable bottle of wine here, all chilled and just waiting for us to open it.'

Gee and I have already agreed to share so mum can have her own room. Ralph follows each of us around, not knowing which way to go next and loving every minute of it. He is here in his favourite place with his special friend just a walk away.

Gee opens the wine and we unpack our cases, get a few bits and pieces together for supper and settle in for an early night. The drive has left me tired but my mind is buzzing with plans for the next day. I'm certain that sleep will not come easily.

Ralph takes himself off to his bed while we're still washing up. Mum takes a cup of hot milk with her up to her room, saying she'll leave us two young things to turn the lights out.

Once we are in bed, Gee is asleep in seconds, but I lay for what seems like forever, tossing and turning. Not wanting to disturb her I get up and go downstairs for a hot drink. I grab a pencil and notebook from my bag. For the last few days phrases and sentences have been forming in my head again, and it's a good feeling, like getting back on a bicycle after recovering from an accident. But nothing will get written just now, because as I reach the foot of the stairs I notice a dim light coming from the kitchen and see that Ralph isn't in his bed.

'Mum, what are you doing up? I thought you'd be worn out after the journey.'

'I could say the same for you,' she says, as she bends down to stroke Ralph.

'Cup of tea?'

'Maybe some warm milk for me, thanks. Emily, you never told me how you and Ralph got together. I don't even know if you have a young man in your life. You don't mention anyone. There's so much of your life I know nothing about. Twenty years of my daughter's life and it's like a blank page.'

I can sense myself bristling, but I'm determined not to go down the old trodden paths of antagonism and bitterness. My mother is reaching out to me, the least I can do is to extend a hand of friendship.

'Ralph found me. I was in a park one day and he happened along and when no-one came to claim him we decided we were meant to be together. I can't imagine my life without him now.'

'Do you know how old he is?'

'He's no spring chicken, but then when he gets the scent of a rabbit he finds his young legs alright. As for a man, well let's just say there's no-one special at the moment.'

'You've had a hard time of it, haven't you?'

'I suppose we've all had hard times. Life hasn't been roses and sunshine for you has it?'

'But I had your father.'

'Yes, he was pretty special. I miss him mum.'

'I know you do. He was very proud of you, Emily. It's a shame he didn't get the chance to tell you.'

I think of that last precious meeting with dad in Brighton, about the two letters he wrote to me that I read over and over until I knew the words by heart. I know he kept his promise and never told mum. Now I can see how unfair I was to ask him to keep it secret. He must have felt so divided.

I watch mum as she bends to stroke Ralph, caressing his ears, and I can sense there's more she wants to say.

'I've never really told you about how your dad and I met, have I?' she says.

'Dad was in the army, wasn't he? Is that when you met?'

A gentle smile spreads over her face, the creases around her eyes making them look youthful and bright.

'If I hadn't got something in my eye that day, then perhaps I would never have met Edgar.'

'In Hastings?'

'Your dad was home on leave. He'd joined up, just turned nineteen. They sent him off for training, then he was allowed back home for a while before joining his battalion.'

'He never talked about the war, mum. Neither of you did.'

She looks beyond me, as if she is trying to travel back to that time in her mind, then she refocuses and smiles.

'I don't recall if it was an eyelash or some sand that blew up as I walked along the promenade. I stopped still, my eye was streaming and I couldn't walk any further. I closed both eyes and before I opened them I felt a hand on my arm. *Pardon me, madam, may I assist you?* he said. A gentle voice, a gentle hand and when I opened one eye I saw the gentlest of faces. Kind eyes. My Edgar's eyes.

'He was in uniform, oh my, he was so smart. He took a clean white handkerchief from his pocket and, using one corner, he carefully wiped away the offending item and with his other hand he was still holding my arm. *There, that should do it,* he said, in a matter of fact way, as though he had just swept the front path and was pleased to see it all looking nice and tidy. *Pleased to meet you, I'm Edgar Carpenter,* he said, holding out a hand to shake mine, forgetting he was still holding the handkerchief.

'*Thank you, Mr Carpenter, you've done me a great service*, I said. *Florence Railton.* I expected him to shake hands and then step back to let me pass and continue on along the promenade. Instead, he continued holding my hand, looking directly at my face.

'*My eye feels very comfortable now*, I told him, *I'm sure there's no further problem. I'll let you get on your way.* And then he says, *You may think me very forward Miss Railton, but would you like to join me for a cup of tea, or better still an ice-cream?* And that was that.'

Mum's face is lit up now, her eyes really sparkling.

'Then when we found out about the baby, well, something like that either pushes you closer together or tears you apart. We relied on each other for everything, but we never talked about your sister. I've made plenty of mistakes in my life, I know that. '

'We all makes mistakes, mum,' I say, taking her hand in mine. For a while we sit in silence. Occasionally I hear the distant sound of an owl hooting.

Then she continues, 'By the time your sister was born your dad was off fighting. And once the war was over we just wanted to be together. He would have made the worst soldier, he couldn't have harmed a single living creature. I kept thinking how lucky I was that he came back to me, that he wasn't killed.'

I recall the photos of dad with his army mates; many of them younger than Thomas is now, sent off to fight a war that would kill millions. I think about all the layers of life that my parents experienced before I was even born.

'Was it a shock when you discovered you were pregnant with me?'

'We didn't think it would ever happen, that it wasn't meant to be. And when you were born your dad was terrified, too scared to hold you, as if you were made of bone china. He'd sit beside me on the settee and gaze at you. After supper and before I put you down for the night, I'd lay you out on my lap and we'd just look at you. Your little nose would wrinkle up as though you were about to sneeze and Edgar would smile and say, *Flo, look at her little nose.* You were six months old before he was brave enough to help bathe you. Until then he'd sit on the chair in the kitchen while I put you in a tub in the sink. You were such a tiny thing. And Edgar would sing to you, little songs he made up about bath time being such fun.

'I'd say to him, *You daft thing, where did you hear that?* And he'd say it just came into his head from nowhere. You'll have got your story writing from him, I'm sure. I was never one for imagining things. Life throws enough at us without having to imagine things that aren't there.'

I remember my childhood bedtimes, when dad would tell me a story, no books, just making it up as he went along.

'He'd call you his precious jewel - do you remember that? And before you came along, that's what I was, his precious jewel. He used to say my eyes were like sapphires. Stuff and nonsense, I'd say, but it was nice to hear all the same.'

I look at mum's eyes now and see them properly for the first time, then I look away for a moment and try to imagine my parents, young and in love.

'The only time I saw your dad cry was the day I told him you were expecting. You asked me to tell your dad, do you remember?'

The memory is as vivid as if it was yesterday. I wanted mum to hug me and tell me it would all be alright, but there was no hug, no reassurance.

'I waited until he and I were in bed that night and when I told him he put his head on my shoulder and wept. *Oh, Flo,* he kept saying, over and over, and I wrapped my arms around him and held him to me. I had to make the decision do you see? I had to make it for both of you. I had to be the strong one.'

I can sense the conversation taking a turn that will lead us down a negative path. I can't think of what to say but I know I have to head her off in another direction.

'You might be right about me getting my love of words from dad. You know I've started writing again.' I open the notebook up and show her the few random notes I've been making over the past few days. 'It's ages since I finished the last book, but as soon as I picked up the pen again it all just started to flow. I'm planning to write about the children who were sent away.'

'About Thomas?'

'About all the children, make it a book to give people a voice, a chance to tell their story.'

It was just after our return from *St Joseph's* when Gee pointed out the same thing to me that Walter had said a few weeks before. I'm a writer. What better way to help all the children whose lives were damaged irrevocably than to write about them, to expose the truth for all to understand?

'And you have a publisher?' mum asks me.

'Yes, Terrence Fortune. Funnily enough, he was my first boss. I met him again at a party recently and found out he publishes non-fiction.'

'And you'll write about what you discover in Australia?'

'That's my hope, mum. My trip to Australia is to find Thomas, but if I can help other people whose lives have been spoiled by narrow-mindedness and short-sighted thinking then I need to grab that chance with both hands.'

As soon as I'd said the words I wanted to take them back.

'Do you mean me?'

'You had your reasons and those were different times. But the decisions people made back then have had a ripple effect.'

She takes a sip of her drink and then looks directly at me.

'We haven't spoken about your sister, since the day I told you; you've never mentioned her.'

I look at my mother, wrapped in a candlewick dressing gown, sipping her warm milk and I try to imagine the young girl. The girl who found she was pregnant and was scared, who had no-one to talk to, no-one who would understand. A girl who had to keep a secret for more than forty years.

'Maybe that's a search we can make together mum, when you're ready?'

'Thank you, Emily.'

'What for?'

'For trying to understand.'

Chapter 29
Anglesey

I wake, stretching my legs out to caress the warm spaces and then move them to enjoy the delight of cooler spots that have remained untouched in the far reaches of my bed. I ease myself out of bed, reaching down to slide my toes into warm slippers.

The weather forecasters warn of a heavy snowfall and recommend people don't travel unless '*absolutely necessary*'. On our walk yesterday the damp ground seemed to have hardened, as though preparing itself for the white covering that will transform it from earth to the brief crystal crispness that reduces us all to children.

It rarely snowed in Hastings, but when it did I couldn't wait to get out into the back garden so that mine were the first footsteps in the fresh blanket that appeared overnight, like magic. I would have rushed out in my slippers I was so keen, but mum fussed around, making sure I had wellington boots, warm hat, scarf and gloves and finally I would be released. I opened the back door and then carefully placed my feet down, one at a time, trying to stretch my stride out as wide as possible so the space in-between remained untouched. Alongside my footprints were delicate tracings in the snow, where birds had landed.

I must have been about eight or nine when we had a really heavy snowfall one winter. The snow had started during the morning and I was at school. It fell so heavily and so quickly that by mid-afternoon the headmistress announced the school would be closing early and we could all go home. My mother usually met me at the end of the school day, but there was no way of contacting her as we didn't have a phone. So, it was up to me to get home on my own. I was terrified. This was a journey I had made with my mum twice a day for three or four years, and yet it was though I had landed in another world, with no route map. I was grateful to have the chance to walk with some of the other children and their parents part of the way, but then for the last half mile or so I was alone. By the time I got home I was cold and tearful. Mum opened the door and told me to go straight upstairs and change out of my cold, wet things and when I got downstairs she had prepared hot, buttered crumpets and a cup of tea. I was allowed to take my plate and sit in front of the crackling fire. Each time I've had crumpets since then, they take me back to that day.

Mum and I sleep in, so by the time we're up and dressed Gee has already prepared breakfast and is raring to go. Ralph is also pacing with anticipation. After breakfast I don my winter boots and even dig out a coat for Ralph, much to his dismay.

'Hold still a minute, will you? If it snows while we're out you'll be grateful for this,' I tell him, as he continues to fidget and I struggle to do up the Velcro fastenings.

The four of us decide to head to the park first, where there is less chance of us slipping over if Ralph decides to launch an attack on a passing cat or squirrel. After an hour or so my fingers are starting to lose all feeling, despite wearing thick gloves. Gee is complaining under her breath about the Welsh weather.

'I think we've had enough now, let's find somewhere to get warm,' I say.

'But promise we'll go up to the cliff-top this afternoon, to track down the elusive Walter. I'm not sure I can wait much longer.'

'Patience my friend, first I want to show you the sights.'

'The sights? I thought this was a sleepy Welsh village.'

'Exactly.'

'Your dad would have loved this place,' mum says. We've stopped off at one of my favourite cafés and I've ordered hot, buttered crumpets for three, plus a biscuit or two for Ralph. 'It reminds me of Hastings fifty years ago.'

'We've been in here an hour,' Gee says. 'By now in Brighton someone would be pushing for your table.'

'I'm looking forward to meeting Gwen and Billy,' mum says. 'She's done so well bringing the boy up on her own after her husband died.'

Gee and I exchange looks. We have our own thoughts about mothers and children and if we voiced them now the gentleness of the mood shared around the table would be broken, so we remain silent.

'Come on,' I say. 'Let's finish up here and wander back. Gwen is expecting us at hers in a few hours.'

A little later we are preparing for tea at Gwen's. She told us not to bring cake as she and Billy have baked one in our honour.

'Let's take flowers then,' mum suggests.

'Or chocolates?' Gee chips in.

'Or both?' I say.

We arrive laden with goodies, to an enthusiastic welcome and hugs all round. Billy takes Ralph straight out into the garden to chase a ball, even though the snow that has fallen over the last couple of hours has covered most of the lawn.

'He's that excited,' Gwen says. 'It's best he works off a bit of energy before tea, or he'll never sit still for long.'

'That goes for Ralph too,' I quip.

A few hours later and we have had our fill of sandwiches and cake and swapped stories about how we all came to know each other. Mum has been quiet, listening contentedly to the chatter and then, as Gwen cuts the celebration cake (a delight of lemon frosting and chocolate buttons) mum asks for our attention.

'I want to say a few words, if you don't mind. I know I'm old and probably a bit dotty, but I'd like to share something with you all.'

I feel my stomach tighten, wondering if this is another revelation and why she has chosen this moment to say it.

'I think I can speak for my daughter and for Geraldine,' she looks at both of us and we each nod, wondering quite what we are agreeing to.

'We've all come a long way to reach this day, not just in miles travelled, but in years too. We've all made mistakes, but all of that has brought us to this point. And it's here that we've had the chance to meet you, Gwen, and your lovely son, Billy. You should be very proud of your son, and he should be proud of his mother. I think the modern vernacular is, *You make a great team.* Thank you for welcoming us into your home and for greeting us as friends.'

Gwen's face flushes and her lip trembles, as she fights off tears. Billy gets up and goes round the table to give my mother a hug.

'We have a new family now mum,' he says. 'It's not just you and me anymore, there's Auntie Geraldine, Miss Emily and...' He pauses, not quite knowing what to say next.

'Grandma Flo,' my mum says and raises her teacup. 'Let's have a toast to family – in all its forms.'

After the celebratory evening we all sleep well and it's only when I hear Ralph padding around downstairs I realise it's time to get up. Today is a big day. For Gee, who has been longing to meet the mysterious Walter, and for me to see the two brothers together again.

I ask mum if she wants to join us up on the cliff top, but she says she prefers to have a quiet morning and that Gwen has promised to pop in. I have a feeling those two will become firm friends.

I've primed Gee and asked her not to bombard Walter with questions.

'I'll behave, I promise,' she says, grinning.

The snow has cleared, leaving a grey slush on the footpaths. I let Ralph lead the way and before long we are winding our way across the headland, approaching Walter's bench.

'It's empty,' Gee says, a note of dismay in her voice.

'Maybe he doesn't come up here now, he's got Patrick remember. It's freezing cold and I'm pretty sure it's not the kind of day he would want to sit around waiting for south coast tourists to happen by. '

'South coast tourists? We're friendly visitors, aren't we? At least you are. Let's sit here for a while and see what happens.'

Sitting on Walter's bench without Walter feels strange. But for the first time it gives me a chance to really take in the view, the one that has drawn him to this place. A sky and seascape that changes colour and shape daily, as the wind blows in and the seasons pass. There are no houses or road to be seen from this vantage point, no reminder of human interference, just nature doing its thing.

We sit in silence for a while and enjoy the peace.

'Are you and Roger talking now?' I ask her.

'We're okay.'

'What about you and Gavin?'

'It's a rift that can't be healed, I'm afraid. Too much history, too many words spoken in anger.'

'He made a mistake, Gee.'

'A mistake that meant I was thrown out of my home, for something that wasn't my fault.'

'Don't you think about your mum and dad, wonder how they are?'

'There's no going back for me, Em, but for you and your mum; from where I'm standing it looks as though you've got the beginnings of a relationship, adult to adult.'

'We've made a start.'

'Will you move here to Anglesey when we are back from Australia?'

'Too early to say.'

'What about your mum? Do you think she will ever move?'

'If you're suggesting we might live together full-time I think that may be a step too far.'

'I get why you like this place. It's funny to see you here, you're different somehow. I'm still too fidgety for such a sleepy place, but for a holiday. I'd come and visit. I can see Roger loving the light for his beloved photography. He's been reading about this new thing; he keeps telling me digital will be all the rage in a few years, whatever that means.'

'Maybe Martha will sell me her cottage.'

'So you're not thinking of a trip to Norfolk? Is it completely over between you and Mark?'

As we chat Ralph lays beneath the bench dozing. But now, as I look down, I see he's raised his head, his ears are alert and his nose is twitching, as if he's picked up the scent of something, or someone. Sure enough, the next thing we hear is Walter's whistle and then he's there standing in front of us and just behind him is Patrick.

'Waiting for someone?' Walter says, smiling.

We stand and Gee holds out her hand and then withdraws it, perhaps feeling a bit daft at offering such a formal greeting. Instead Walter takes her hand and holds it in his.

'Hello, you must be Geraldine. I see you've been taking in the beauty of this place.'

I look at him, wondering what point he's making. With Walter there is always another meaning.

'I've been watching you for a while. You both look relaxed. Looks like Anglesey is working its magic.'

'Geraldine has been dying to meet you.'

'I'm honoured to have been the subject of your conversation.'

'She loves a mystery does Gee, and you, the way you live, the reason you chose this place, it all intrigues her.'

'I'm not such an unusual case. We all choose to settle somewhere and we all have our own reasons.'

'We're going to Australia,' Gee says, unable to contain herself any longer.

'To find Thomas?'

I nod, looking at Patrick. 'I know it may not give me the answers I want, but at least I won't have regrets that I didn't try.'

'Emily is determined to let the world know what happened to children like you, Patrick. She's going to write a book to tell people the truth of it all.' Gee directs her gaze at Patrick. 'So even if we can't find Thomas, maybe the book will help another soul with their search.'

'Did you meet Marjorie?' Patrick asks.

'She's a wonder,' I say. 'But there's so many people who need help, she must feel overwhelmed at times.'

'Your book will help, I'm sure. She'll be grateful for that,' Walter says, watching for Patrick's reaction.

'It will shine a light on some of the travesties that have occurred over decades,' Gee says.

'Travesties? That's a strong word.'

'Injustices then. Can we tell your story, Walter? Yours and Patrick's?' As Gee continues I feel more and more uncomfortable. I understand Walter's desire for privacy, it's something that has been precious for me for years. At least a privacy of sorts. Until Jocelyn's published interview only a handful of people knew anything about my private life and I liked it that way. Telling people about yourself opens you up to judgement and criticism.

'My story is not so different. I'm luckier than many and now I have Lloyd back in my life, I'm complete.'

'Have you found somewhere to stay?' I want to ask so many questions, but that is not the pattern of our friendship. Walter has taught me to listen.

'Anglesey is our home now,' Patrick says. 'Anna has found a job looking after the local photographic studio, she's in her element, her boss is even going to teach her a few things about photography. She reckons she's headed for fame and fortune.'

We all walk together while Patrick tells us a little more about their immediate plans. 'Walter and I are working together on a local farm, they didn't even notice my limp. It seems it's hard to get good honest workers wherever you go. And my brother is right, this place is as close to the outback as I reckon you'll get this side of the world. We've got space, freedom and family. I don't think we need anything else.'

'Will we see you tomorrow, Walter?' I ask him as we reach the end of the footpath.

'I hope so,' he says.

Chapter 30
Melbourne, Australia

We spend our time in Anglesey walking, talking and enjoying the company of friends and family and that's not something I would have thought possible when I started the search for my son. But Thomas is still out there somewhere and now all I want is to find him.

Our trip to Australia is planned. We ask Roger to keep an eye on Ralph (or, as Gee suggested, it might be the other way around). I book flights, with a stopover at Singapore. I doubt either of us would cope without an overnight break.

'Our legs are too long,' I explain to Roger.

'I bet that's the first time the travel agent has heard that excuse.'

Ten days later we're packed and Roger is taking us through our last-minute checklist.

'Passports, tickets, money?'

'Check.'

'Hostel address?

'Check.'

'Sun cream, sunglasses, bikinis.'

'Bikinis? Are you kidding? We're almost middle aged and we don't want to scare the locals. Okay, now it's my turn. What time does Ralph have supper?'

'6pm sharp.'

'Yes, and no treats in the evening or he'll get fat. And don't forget to check him for ticks when you come back from your walks, especially if you've been in the long grass. I mean if he's been in the long grass.'

'Ralph, don't you wish their flight was this evening, then you and I can get down to the serious business of relaxing and enjoying ourselves?'

Ralph responds by jumping onto the sofa and setting his head down firmly on Roger's knee.

'Sorry, separation anxiety,' I say. 'I know you'll be fine, I mean I know he'll be fine. Gee can worry about you.'

'Worry about him?' she says, smirking. 'No chance. Once I'm on that plane I won't give him a second thought,'

'What it is to be loved, or should that be what is it to be loved?' Roger says, grinning.

'Well, if absence really does make the heart grow fonder then you'll be all over each other once we're back and Ralph and I will be walking the coastline of Britain to stay out of your hair.'

'A touch extreme, but maybe the South Downs Way for starters?' Roger says, stroking Ralph's ears.

Roger drives us to the airport and Ralph keeps his head on my leg throughout the journey, as if he's claiming possession. He has seen the suitcases go into the boot and he's no fool.

'Make the goodbyes short or I'll have a whining dog on my hands the whole way back to Brighton. I'm going to pull up in the drop-off zone, the car parking is extortionate.'

Gee grabs a baggage trolley and Roger loads our cases onto it. I give Ralph a kiss on his head, and Roger a hug and then push the trolley towards the airport entrance while Gee and Roger say their goodbyes.

As we walk along the travelator into the terminal we are silent, absorbing the sounds around us. Two young children running hand in hand pass us, followed by their parents struggling to keep up, while wheeling cases and pushchairs laden with bags and toys. A young couple stand ahead of us gazing at each other, perhaps off on their first holiday together, or their honeymoon. As we come to the end of the travelator there is a loud beeping and we look behind to see an electric buggy coming towards us carrying five elderly passengers, each looking a little apprehensive.

'I love airports,' Gee says.

'You sound like a seasoned traveller. How many times have you been in an airport, Geraldine O'Connell?'

'Um three, no four. Weekend trip to Paris, fortnight in Majorca, week in Corfu and city break to Rome. Anyway, we've got ages to wait, let's stand at arrivals for a while, watch the faces of the people coming through. Try to guess if they're coming home or if their adventure is just beginning.'

A single man arrives, wearing a Stetson, but looking like a lost cowboy. Some priests come through in a group, each looking through the waiting crowd for a familiar face, a sign, not from God, but one that is roughly handwritten to indicate they are expected.

Wherever you look, airport staff are busy; one young man, dressed in uniform, his hair carefully covered with a cap, empties waste bins; another is sweeping. And then there's the air crew, hostesses with their slim, trim figures, poised, with perfect make-up, hair neat, and uniforms freshly pressed, and the pilots, walking with authority.

All the cafés and bars are full, each table spilling over with empty cups, half-eaten sandwiches. People eating when they are not hungry, all looking for a way of passing the time, eking out the endless wait.

We pass through customs and passport control and spend a while perusing the duty-free shop.

'Shall we get a bottle of vodka to keep in our room at the hostel - for those nights when we need to drown our sorrows?' Gee says, checking the special offer prices.

'How about perfume?'

'Doesn't work as well as alcohol and doesn't taste as good. Anyway, we're not on the pull remember?'

'Put your purse away, let's just get some sweets for the journey and go and grab a coffee. We've got two hours to kill before our flight.'

After coffee and a sandwich we find a seat and people watch for a while.

'I love airports,' Gee says.

'I think we've already had this conversation.'

The first hour of the flight is exciting. We are setting off across the world and everything we experience is new and fresh. We relax into our seats, which are more comfortable than I imagined and play with the TV screen, plugging in the headphones and exploring what's on offer. The senior stewardess announces that we can ask for drinks at any time and that meals will be served shortly. Once we are up and away the pilot reports on the flying conditions in a reassuring tone. It's a well-oiled operation and after take-off there is so little movement in the plane it's easy to forget we are thirty-eight thousand feet above the ground.

I work my way through a couple of films, interspersed with food, drinks and magazine browsing. I've brought a book that I've been wanting to read for ages, hoping this will be the perfect opportunity, hours and hours of undisturbed reading. But two pages in and I realise that my mind is wandering. I am standing in baking heat with a line of young men in front of me, each of them with accusing stares. I have to choose one from the line-up, the one that is my flesh and blood.

'Are you okay, you're sweating. Look, pull out that little black thing over your head. It's fresh air.' Gee points to the air-conditioning vent above me.

'I doubt it's fresh,' I say.

I put the book away and switch the TV monitor back on, flicking through the channels, searching for any distraction.

'We will be landing in Singapore in ten minutes. The temperature is a comfortable 27 degrees and it's quite cloudy, but you will be pleased to know it's not raining, at least not at present. Please remain in your seats and fasten your seat belts.'

We've been told to expect thunderstorms in Singapore and have come prepared with lightweight macs and the traditional British umbrella. Roger thought it was hysterical.

'I'm going to take a photo of this, packing an umbrella to go to Australia. You two are an embarrassment to all English travellers.'

'It's for Singapore. There may be the odd shower.'

'Sounds about right, you two are an odd shower.'

When we finally arrive in Melbourne the throng of people in the arrivals hall is almost suffocating. We stand at the baggage reclaim belt and watch luggage move steadily round and round, appearing then disappearing, only to reappear again if uncollected. The cases are like the people, all shapes and sizes. Some of the luggage is colour co-ordinated, other bags are battered and uncertain as to whether to stand upright or tip over, falling close to the edge of the belt. It reminds me of a game show - make your choice as gifts pass you by.

I've marked my case with a tartan ribbon, tied in a neat bow on the handle.

'It'll make it easier to spot,' I told Gee.

If only my search for Thomas could be granted the same success. If my child, now a man, could wear a badge that clearly indicates him as mine and mine alone. When I replay those days, just after the birth, each time I rewrite the story. Sometimes I give him a gift, a small St Christopher medal to hang around his tiny neck. The medal engraved on the reverse, says, *With love from your mother, Emily Carpenter.* Then he would always know me. He would keep the medal, take it out now and again throughout his life and know that he was loved. That he is loved.

On other occasions, when I am replaying the recording in my head, he is not taken away from me. Instead he is put into my arms and I sit, cradling his tiny body, holding him gently, rocking him to and fro. Then I remember the truth of it and find myself rocking, backwards and forwards, as though I am the baby and he is gone.

Chapter 31
Melbourne, Australia

We take a taxi into the city and find the hostel, which is heaving with young backpackers.

'We should have done this in our youth, Em, we'd have had a ball.'

'One minor point - no money. And hitching to Oz might have been tricky?' I say.

'Point taken.'

'Anyway, we're still in our youth, kind of.'

'Absolutely. How about him, for example.' Gee points at a tall blond-haired lad. 'He's a dish.'

'Having a ball does not mean getting laid. But yes, he's a dish and young enough to be your son.'

'Or yours.'

I am no longer smiling.

'My big mouth. Can I blame it on jet lag this time?'

'Come on, let's check in, then make a start. We've got a lot to cover.'

We've already planned to visit the newspaper office as a first port of call. Patrick has told us as much as he can about *The Farm*, but we know we can't just turn up there. We hope that someone at the newspaper office will have had feedback from the advert that Marjorie placed that might give us some leads, even put us in touch with other boys or girls like Patrick.

Ernest White, the advertising manager, is intrigued. Two English women arriving in his office is clearly no common occurrence and he wants to know more.

'That was a private ad,' is all Ernest will tell us. 'What's it to you anyway?'

'Mr White,' explains Gee, in her most persuasive tone. 'We've travelled all the way from England. The thing is we saw your advert, the advert in your paper, and we wondered if it might help us with a search of our own.'

'How's that?' Ernest asks.

'The truth is Mr White,' Gee continues, 'we've learned that some children who were in care in England were transported to Australia in the decades after the war, right up until the late 1960s and we'd like to know a bit more about it. Who they were and how it all happened.'

'Sounds pretty unlikely. Anyways the woman who placed the ad would be the one to ask. She's asked for people to contact her direct.'

He opens the door and indicates the meeting is over. He wants us out.

'That was a waste of time,' I say, while we are still within earshot of the unhelpful Mr White. But I am past caring about his sensibilities.

'Don't give up at the first hurdle,' Gee says. 'You're made of stronger stuff than that. Come on, let's grab a coffee and make a plan.'

We hover outside his office for a few moments, looking around at the rest of the newspaper staff.

'Okay,' Gee says, 'what are our options?'

'Limited.'

'No, we need to think laterally. We could put our own advert in the paper, we're looking for family, aren't we?'

'Who do we think we're kidding, Gee? This is such a long shot. We can't even identify the haystack, let alone the needle.'

'One step at a time, trust me.'

'I do trust you, it's just all incredibly daunting and such a muddle. This is a big country and the ships didn't just come into Melbourne. Thomas may have arrived in Perth, or...'

'Like I say, one step at a time.'

We are about to leave the building when the receptionist stops us. Speaking in hushed tones she presses a piece of paper into my hand.

'This is a list of the people who have responded to the advert so far. Names and phone numbers. I don't have addresses. But I'll lose my job if anyone finds out I told you. It's just that if it's true, the rumours, then it's too bad and someone needs to help these people.'

We leave with even more questions in our heads, but we don't want to push her anymore, and are grateful she's given us a starting point. We work our way methodically down the list until the fifth phone call leads us to a man called Ian. Gee, with her gift for storytelling (she should have been the author) explains we are here from England. We let him jump to a few conclusions. I guess he thinks we'd placed the original ad, or at least that we're connected to the person who had. He is grateful for the chance to meet us.

His quiet voice on the phone leads us to expect a man with a diminutive physique, instead this fifty-year-old is burly and bronzed. He reminds me of one of dad's favourite actors from the westerns of the 1950s, raw and ready to tackle any sharp shooter who crosses him. But Ian's demeanour is as far from a rough, tough cowboy as it's possible to be. He struggles to have eye contact with either Gee or me, keeping his head permanently bent, his eyes looking downwards. As I shake his hand he holds mine for a few moments, as though he's trying to assess my character, my intentions.

We meet by an outside coffee kiosk and stand side by side; he looks as awkward as I feel. We tell him the truth about our reasons for coming to Australia, for getting in touch with him. We avoid any mention of the kind Rosalie from the newspaper office. He seems happy to trust us and is grateful to find someone to listen to his story.

We recount some of our conversations with Patrick, explaining that his story led us to Australia to find out more. After spending an hour or so with him, we arrange a second meeting and Ian offers to take us to the place where he grew up. It isn't until we pull up at the end of the mile-long drive and see the sign above the entrance that we realise this is *The Farm* Patrick told us about.

We stand looking up at a pair of ornate wrought iron gates, opening onto a long drive. Either side of the gates is a high stone wall, meaning our only view of what lies beyond is through the woven ironwork. A man dressed in sombre attire greets us at the gate.

Ian shakes the man's hand, the gates are opened and we walk through. The man walks ahead of us, with no introductions, leaving us to talk undisturbed.

'We created the road you're walking on, cleared the rocks and shovelled sand, tons of it,' Ian says.

Gee and I look at each other, unable to find an appropriate response.

'All the boys worked on these paths, that wall too.' He points at a long wall about four foot high, running the full length of the path. 'We made each brick by hand. We mixed the sand and cement together and then used a machine to press them into shape.'

It's impossible to comprehend what this man is telling us. For all that Patrick has shared with us, being faced with the reality is hard to take.

'They'd sit and watch us,' he says, nodding towards the man who had let us in, who is now hovering up ahead out of earshot. 'They'd drink tea while we worked. Some of the boys didn't make it through,' Ian says, his tone is reverent. 'It was hardest for the little ones. When they first arrived from England their skin was pale. The sun burnt them badly and they'd cry, but they soon learned not to cry. The beatings weren't the worst of it.' He avoids our gaze, as though he is ashamed.

We continue on down the long, dusty drive, past ornate buildings.

'These buildings weren't here when I first arrived. I was ten when I got here.'

'You came from England when you were ten?'

He nods. 'I was here six years and in that time us boys built a lot of what you see here.'

'I don't understand,' I say, as I try to imagine what the children were forced to do. But as the images form in my mind I realise I don't want to imagine any of it.

'In England I was used to houses and streetlights,' Ian continues. 'Here there were just trees and open fields and the nights were black. You could be out here on a cloudy night and not even see the ground you're standing on.'

'Did you ever try to leave?' Gee asks.

'Some of the boys tried to run away,' Ian continues, looking at the ground as he speaks. 'There were stories, but you never knew how many were true. We heard one of the boys stole a rifle and ended up shooting himself rather than get caught. But, like I say, you never knew what to believe. We never saw him again anyway.'

'Ian, if this is too much for you, stirring up painful memories…' I say, wondering whether it is my own sensibilities I am trying to protect.

'The memories don't need no stirring,' he says. 'Some people have memories of family, they know who they are, where they came from. I know my mum put me into a children's home near Liverpool after dad died. She thought I'd be better off without her. Then, when they sent me here, they told me she was dead.'

'Do you think it's true? Have you tried to trace your family? Is there anyone who can help you?'

Ian shakes his head.

'Patrick, the young man we told you about, he was here at *The Farm*, but years after you left, he's just twenty now. He's travelled to England and he's managed to find his brother. Maybe you have family too, someone who is looking for you? The woman who placed the advert in the *Melbourne Herald*, she's coming over here soon. Maybe she can help you.'

'There are so many of us, we all want the same thing. I'd just like to know the truth, whatever it is. I'm pleased for your friend Patrick though. It's good to hear he's found his brother.'

We continue to walk and Ian seems keen to keep talking.

'One of my friends, Larry, he was up on scaffolding one day and was given a backhander 'cos he wasn't working hard enough. He fell down onto some concrete, broke his back. He tried to get up and walk, but then he collapsed. They just put him in the sick room, no doctor, nothing. Then a few days later they must have thought better of it and they transferred him to hospital. He was in there for weeks, and we weren't allowed to visit. Every time I asked how he was I was told to mind my own business. Larry was told he'd never walk again, but he was a fighter. I remember the day he came out of hospital, I was so glad to see him. He walked right into the dormitory, he had a bad limp mind you, but there he was walking and I got a clip round the ear for getting up off my chair to go and shake his hand.'

Gee and I look at each other. I wonder how many boys like Patrick and Larry have had to suffer these abominations in silence. Suddenly I need to sit, afraid that I will faint. Gee sits beside me on the ground, ground ingrained with the sweat, blood and tears of young children.

'Why?' Gee says.

'Because they could,' is Ian's simple reply.

'I'd like to leave now,' I say, slowly coming to standing.

'Thank you, Ian,' Gee says, as she holds his hand in both of hers and the three of us turn to go back through the gates, leaving *The Farm* behind us.

We have been quiet since our return to the hostel. Finally breaking the silence, Gee says, 'This is where Patrick grew up, maybe Thomas was here as well. Em, let's go to the authorities, see what records they have. They must have known something about these children who crossed the world to bump up their workforce.'

'Yes, and why do you think for a moment they would want to tell us anything?'

'Let's threaten them. Tell them we're with the media, journalists or something.'

'Someone's already tried that, remember. I think we should give up and go home.'

'Emily, when have you ever known me to give up?'

'Just tell me this, who decided to call these places 'care homes'? Perhaps a lesson in definition wouldn't go amiss.'

My thoughts turn to my dad's dictionary. Which definition would I choose? *'Care'* is *'painstaking, watchful attention'* - someone who is cared for is *'the subject of attention, anxiety or solicitude.'*

'*The Farm* is a perfect name for that place,' Gee replies, 'somewhere children were treated like animals.'

We spend the next few days trawling through library archives to see if we can find any mention of the child migrants. We read through many reference books, old newspapers and journals, but none of it is what we are looking for. When we get back to the hostel on the third day, we sit out in the garden with a couple of cans of lemonade.

'From everything we've read so far, I reckon there are some parts of Australian history they don't want to be reminded of,' Gee says.

'Did your folks ever think of going out there from Ireland? It's incredible to think over a million families took up that '*ten pound poms*' scheme.

'There's no way my mum and dad would have even discussed it, they're too entrenched in Ireland to ever leave.'

'It's funny to think of all the ways the Australian authorities thought of to fill up an empty country. Because that's pretty much what they did, isn't it?'

'Well, they had the Gold Rush, didn't they? That brought people in from all over, not just Europe, but America and China.

Families making choices was one thing, but what Ian and Patrick have told us about is a story of children forcibly transferred, with many providing slave labour for groups of people who purported to be philanthropists and do-gooders. There was no evidence that British authorities checked on the welfare of the migrant children. More than that, it appeared that this was a policy that was to remain hidden, swept under the proverbial carpet.

We finish our cans of drink and as I stand to head back into the hostel, I sense Gee wants to say something.

'Let's go back to *The Farm*, quiz them, force them to give us names and dates.'

When I don't answer, she admits that all she really wants is to have a shouting match with the men who purported to be holier than thou, who instead should be begging for forgiveness from their Creator.

'This is the closest we've been to finding Thomas, Em.'

'You go if you want to, I can't face it,' I tell her. 'But you'll be wasting your time. They won't tell us a thing. Why should they?'

Despite the threat of mosquitoes, I've slept with the window open and my early morning alarm call is birdsong. Walter told me to listen out for birds that were just native to Australia. He challenged me to try to remember their call; I try to repeat it in my mind now, but am certain that I will have forgotten it by the time I see him again. Anglesey will be in the throes of late autumn, wild, wet and windy and I imagine Walter and Patrick bundled up against the weather, as they plough furrows in farmland, clearing the land ready for winter sowing.

Gee is already up and as I walk downstairs to the little dining area to join her for breakfast I am reminded that once again I am being selfish.

'Morning,' I say and sit beside her at the rough wooden table. 'I've done it again, haven't I?'

'I know you're scared, but then so was Thomas when they put him on that boat.'

'I know, sorry.'

'You don't need to say sorry, none of this is your fault, or my fault, or your mum's fault come to that. We're all victims, but the children are the real victims and we need to fight for them. Even though we're years too late to fix things. What do you say?'

'Lead the way,' I say, 'I'm ready.'

Ian had said we could contact him anytime and that he would be pleased to take us on another visit to *The Farm*. This time he comes over to the hostel to meet us. We sit outside under the shade of a spreading red cedar tree and listen as he explains to us a little more about his life since leaving *The Farm*.

'I've been lucky really,' he says. 'I've always found work and just recently they've asked me if I want to go back to *The Farm* to work. But I can't do it, no matter that the place is quite different now. Inside my head it's still the same.'

'They want you to work there? That's pretty ironic, isn't it?'

'They do good things now, they help young people, kids who are struggling to get on in life, disadvantaged I suppose you'd call them. They give them training, that kind of thing.'

'What, to make up for the lives they've already ruined?' Gee doesn't attempt to hide her anger.

'It's hard to let go of the memories, but at least there's some good work being done now. I'm grateful for that.'

'Do you think they'd talk to us?' I ask him. We tell Ian more about our search for Thomas. 'We know it's a long shot, but someone must know what happened to him when he got off that ship.'

'I'll do whatever I can to help you. One of the chaps who works there now is easy to talk to, his name's Oliver Haywood. Maybe we can start with him and see how we get on.'

This time when we reach *The Farm* I look again at the road and the buildings that Ian and children like him had toiled over. I wonder what scars Thomas might have, both inside and out.

We are introduced to Oliver, who is happy to take us through to an office, lined with filing cabinets. He sees me looking at the cabinets and shakes his head.

'Miss Carpenter, I'm guessing that the information you are hoping for relates to children who were here many years ago, before we were a therapeutic training centre?'

I have many harsh words to say in reply, but I say nothing and just smile.

'All the files here relate to the young people we are working with at the moment, but we do have archives. Ian tells me you are trying to trace your son, he's called Thomas, is that right? Thomas Carpenter?'

'Yes, Mr Haywood, his name is Thomas Carpenter and he arrived here in Australia when he was five years old. But I'm not holding out much hope that you can help me.'

'I will do what I can, but I'm not making any promises. I think you might understand already that names weren't always…'

'Yes, we know all about names being changed and birth certificates being falsified,' Gee intervenes. I look at her and shake my head. We need to keep this man onside, this is not the time for accusations. We give him as much information as we have about Thomas.

'He was transferred from *St Joseph's* children's home in Brighton, England in 1972. He would have had his fifth birthday on the ship. We don't know much more. We don't even know if he ended up in Melbourne. Some of the children went to Perth, didn't they?'

'Leave it with me for a few days and I'll see what I can find out. Fifteen years have passed, so…'

'I know what you're thinking and you need to stop it now,' Gee says as we take a walk around the gardens of the hostel that evening.

'If I'd done something before now, Gee, it might have…'

'Stop. No more ifs and buts. We are where we are and you need to trust in fate, which is exactly what dear Walter would tell you if he was here.'

Chapter 32
Melbourne, Australia

He knows I'm coming and he has agreed to meet me, for which I'm more than grateful. I've asked Gee to wait outside. This is one meeting I have to do alone. I open the little white gate and walk up the neatly laid path to a front door that is set back inside a timber porch. The bungalow is wide, standing in the centre of an even wider plot. On each side of the property are thick hedges, a mix of red and green, all carefully trimmed and shaped.

A child's football is sitting on the front lawn and I can hear a splashing sound coming from the back garden, where I guess some of the family are enjoying a swim.

Oliver called us at the hostel yesterday to tell us he'd set up a meeting. I knew there would be no point in trying to sleep last night. Instead I wrote letters to each of the people who have travelled this journey with me.

To Mark I write to thank him for helping me realise I'd been hiding from myself for years. He didn't know about the Emily who had left another life behind when she was just sixteen, because I'd hidden that person away, buried her under a cover of pretence and busyness.

I wrote to my darling Gee to thank for always believing in me, with everything that has entailed over twenty years.

The letter to my mum and dad was difficult to get just right. I know now it was only their love for me that led them to make the choices they made. I read the letter aloud, hoping my dad will hear it, wherever he is.

As I write to Walter and Patrick I think again about the wonder of that reunion, how the ties that join people are sometimes too strong ever to be broken apart.

My last letter is to Thomas. I have it now in my pocket as I walk up the path and knock gently on the front door.

The door opens and there stands a handsome young man, tall and bronzed, with chocolate brown eyes. I'm reminded of my father's words, *Do you think he's got Emily's eyes?* he asked my mum. I want to shout out, *Yes, look dad, here's your grandson.*

'Pleased to meet you,' Thomas says and holds out his hand. I take his hand in mine and hold it there, feeling the warmth and strength in it. 'Will you come in and meet my mum and dad?'

I flinch, but smile. 'Yes, of course, thank you.' I follow him along the long corridor into a wide open sitting room, with huge picture windows overlooking the back garden. Two young children are splashing about in the pool, which fills one half of the garden.

'Pleased to meet you,' an older man steps forward and shakes my hand.

I feel divided, I don't know whether to sit or stand, smile or cry. The journey has been long and many times I thought it would end with me standing in a graveyard, putting flowers beside a headstone, commemorating a life half lived. Instead, Thomas is here, in front of me, strong, healthy, living in a beautiful house and thriving as part of a loving family.

I am offered a drink, cold or hot, the older man asks. I tell him water is fine and all the while I sense Thomas watching me. At this point a woman enters the room, she introduces herself as Marion. She is poised, serene even. I need to explain, to apologise and yet my sense of shame is mixed with anger. This could have been me, this should have been me.

She shakes my hand and then sits beside her husband, both of them opposite me, with Thomas to my left. This is no circle and could never be one.

Marion starts to speak, she asks a few questions, have I been to Australia before, have I travelled alone. General niceties, which at their heart reinforce the chasm that lies between the child I gave birth to twenty years before and the young man now sitting a few feet away from me.

'Oliver Haywood tells us you're researching a book,' Marion says, 'you're telling the stories of some of the children who came here from England, is that right?'

I don't know how to reply. Never have I needed Gee more than at this moment. Oliver had told me that he hadn't given the Durhams the real reason for my visit, he suggested it was up to me to share my story if I chose to.

'Yes,' I say, 'I'm writing a book. I've learned that some of them had a hard time of it.'

Walter's voice is ringing in my ears, *Don't ask questions, unless you are prepared to hear the answers.*

Thomas is shuffling his feet and takes a breath as though he's about to speak.

'Thomas knows all about how he came to us,' Marion says. 'We've always told him the truth, as soon as he was old enough to understand. He knows he was born in England, but then as soon as he arrived here he came to live with us.'

My hands have been closed tightly into fists, but now they relax a little.

'Some of the children stayed at *The Farm,* but some of them, like Thomas, were chosen by families like us. We couldn't have a child of our own, but it was God's plan. He sent Thomas to us and he's as much our son as if I'd given birth to him.'

In all the years I've thought about this moment I never imagined it would be as difficult as this. I realise I've lived with pretence for twenty years, imagining the tidy resolution of something that will always be in fragments.

'Thomas was five years old when he arrived here in Australia. He was too little to remember his birth parents, he would have been just a toddler when they died.'

I am being kicked and the bruises will never heal. I try to calm my breathing so that my voice does not give me away. 'Do you remember your journey from England, Thomas?' I look at my son and wonder how I will walk away today, how I will get on the plane and return to England, leaving behind the part of me I've missed for so long.

'Not really,' he says. 'I have fuzzy memories, but just shapes and sounds, the ship's horn blasting, people rushing around. I remember the cake though, at least I'm pretty sure the memory is real.'

'Thomas was on the ship for his fifth birthday,' Marion says. 'He has a memory of eating a birthday cake with some of the other children. We don't know how likely it is though, that he'd have been packed off with a cake in his bag.'

I remember the image of Sister Luke, with her party hat perched on her wispy, grey hair, recalling the little boy who shared her birthday.

Until now Marion's husband has remained silent, but now he stands, as if to make his words carry more weight. 'We've been good parents.'

'Don't start, Stu. Miss Carpenter doesn't want to hear you ranting on.' Marion puts her hand on her husband's arm, encouraging him to sit down.

'I'm just saying,' he continues. 'I've heard stories, things that people are saying. Maybe it's true, maybe it's not. But we've looked after Thomas like our own, given him a good life. Isn't that right, Tom?'

'Calm down, dad, the lady isn't accusing anyone of anything. What kind of stories are you planning to put in your book, Miss? My life hasn't been much different from any other fella, I reckon. It's just that I had those first few years in England, but this is my home and this is my family.'

There's nowhere for me to go. I can't tell this gentle couple the truth. I can't tell Thomas that he's been lied to by the authorities, that his mother didn't die, that she's alive and sitting beside him.

'You've been so kind, but I ought to be going now. I've taken up enough of your time,' I say. I need air, I need Gee to steady the tumult that fills my head.

'You're very welcome,' Marion says. 'I ought to be getting those kids out of the pool now anyway. They live a few doors away, but their pool's out of action. Their mum will be picking them up soon and she'll be wanting them dry and dressed. If you think we can help with anything else, feel free to call again,' she says, as she walks me to the door.

Chapter 33
Melbourne, Australia

I want to run as far and as fast I can. I want my dad to put his arms around me and tell me it will all be alright. Gee has been waiting in a little café two streets away. She is sitting by the window and watches me approach.

'Oh God, it was bad, wasn't it?' she says as she gives me a hug. 'Sit and drink coffee and tell me what happened.'

I explain, struggling to find the words to describe how I am feeling.

'I feel wrung out and yet numb at the same time, if that's possible. '

'Hey, anything is possible with what you've just been through. I'm so proud of you, Emily Carpenter.'

'Why on earth would you feel proud of me?'

'Because you've put Thomas and Marion and Stu first. You've held back from telling them the one thing you must have wanted to shout from the rooftops.'

'But where do I go from here, Gee? I can't just walk away. I've come so far and yet if I leave without him knowing the truth, then it's all been worthless.'

'Let's unpick this, shall we? What did you hope for your son?'

'That he is well and that he's had a good life.'

'We can tick those boxes then, can't we? What else?'

'That he's known love.'

'We've scored a hit there too. So what else is there? The rest is what you want for yourself.'

'I'm being selfish again, is that what you're saying?'

'No, I'm saying that you're allowed to want something for yourself.'

'I want a relationship with my son. I want to be part of his life. Is that wrong?'

'I might have the answer. Good job your friend is a genius.'

When I return to the house this time Gee comes with me. It may be the only time she meets my son. Over tea and cake I gently explain my connection to Thomas's mother. After a few moments' silence while the three of them digest the news, Thomas says, 'So, you're my aunt? My birth mother was your sister?'

I nod. I wonder what my mother would think of this lie. I hope she will understand it's told with love.

'What was she like, my mum?'

'She was…' I'm not prepared. I knew this would be hard, but watching his face filled with hope, I wonder if I've done the right thing.

'Your mother was a very brave person,' Gee says.

'You knew her too?'

'Yes, Thomas, I knew her very well.' Gee continues. 'She was kind, generous and clever.'

'What about my dad?'

'He played the guitar,' I say.

'Did he really? I've been thinking about learning to play, so maybe I'll be okay at it. Was he good?'

I'm aware that Marion and Stu haven't said anything until now, but have been holding hands, watching Thomas.

'We always wondered about his English family, why no-one had got in touch, we guessed there was no-one left who knew about him,' Marion says.

I realise what she is asking.

'The truth of it is we didn't know Thomas had come to Australia,' I explain. 'When his birth parents…' I hesitate, it feels wrong to talk about Johnny as if he's dead, when I hope he's living happily somewhere, oblivious of all that has happened since that teenage romance.

'We couldn't look after Thomas, so he was put into a children's home,' I feel better now I'm on steady ground, keeping as close to the truth as possible. 'The children's home decided to send some of the children to Australia, but we weren't told. It's taken us until now to find out the truth.'

'We haven't done anything wrong,' Stu says, 'we just offered a home to an orphan boy. We didn't know he had family still living.'

'Please Mr Durham, we really are not here to apportion any blame. We're thrilled we've found Thomas and that he's in a loving family. You've brought him up to be a fine young man and I'm sure you are very proud of him,' Gee says.

'Do I have any other relatives in England?' Thomas asks. 'Have I got any cousins.'

I think about the sister I may never meet, the children she may have, nephews, nieces.

'You have a grandmother,' I say, 'her name is Florence. Sadly, your grandfather died a few months ago. He was a very special man, you would have got on well together.'

'It's a lot to take in. It's funny though, when you came here the other day, when I met you the first time, I felt as though I'd met you before. I've never had a feeling like that, as if there's a connection somehow. It sounds strange, I know.'

'No, Thomas, it doesn't sound strange at all.'

'Tom, why don't you take your aunt into the garden, it'll give you the chance to talk a while.' Marion stands and beckons to Gee. 'Maybe you'd like to help me with the dishes?'

I follow Thomas out into the garden. Just to the side of the swimming pool is a covered seating area. It offers some shade and he gestures to me to sit, but he remains standing. He takes a deep breath and I sense he wants to say something, but is searching for the words.

'You're a good person,' he says, finally.

I look at him, knowing there is more to come.

'You don't want to upset Marion and Stu, but I think you owe me the truth.'

I look up at my son, the bright sunlight makes me squint. The words are hovering inside my head, but it's as though they are too scared to land onto my lips. Once they are spoken they will change everything.

'You're not my aunt, are you?' he says, holding my gaze. 'I'm not angry, I don't blame you. I know whatever you did you had your reasons.'

'I've always loved you,' I say, hoping that is enough.

We go back inside to find Gee chatting to Marion and Stu as though she has known them forever.

'How much longer are you in Australia?' Thomas asks, as we prepare to leave.

'Just a few more days. Maybe we can meet up again before we leave, if that's alright with your mum and dad?' I look at Marion for reassurance and she smiles and nods.

'Tom would like that,' she says, as she shakes my hand.

When we arrive at Melbourne airport and check in our bags, someone taps me on the shoulder. It seems that Gee has told Thomas the day and time of our departure and now he stands in front of me. I give my son a hug, an experience I never believed I'd have, just a few months ago.

'You will always be welcome to stay with us if you make it to England,' I say. 'I know it's a long way, but…'

'I've already talked to mum and dad about it,' he says, stumbling a little over the words, 'they're going to help me with the fare. I'll need to save up for a while, but I'll write to you, let you know.'

I'm going to receive a letter from my son. I think of the letter I've written him, the one I still have in my pocket.

'I'll write to you too, if that's okay?' I say.

'We need to go through to departures now,' Gee says, gently taking my arm.

As we walk through the security check I turn to wave. Thomas smiles and waves and as he runs his fingers through his ebony quiff, I see Johnny.

'You would be proud of our son,' I whisper, before Thomas disappears out of sight among the crowds.

Afterword

When I first learned about the child migrants I was shocked and saddened. At the time I was working on my Masters in Professional Writing. I was compelled to do something to raise awareness and made a commitment to do just that.

I went on to read all I could about the Child Migrants Trust, as well as any published accounts from child migrants. I watched the film *Oranges and* Sunshine and scoured newspaper archives for background. I also had the opportunity to visit the Immigration Museum in Melbourne to learn more about the history of immigration to Australia, in all its forms.

But the book that started it all for me was Margaret Humphreys' own harrowing account. In her book, *Empty Cradles (Oranges and Sunshine)* she explains how she first came to discover the truth about the policy of sending children across the world to British colonies. She recounts some of the stories she heard first-hand from those children, now adults. It makes for harrowing reading. Margaret has dedicated many years of her life to try to mend families that have been broken apart by this policy. She set up the Child Migrants Trust (https://www.childmigrantstrust.com/) and since 1986 has helped thousands of people to trace their origins.

She discovered that some 130,000 children were sent overseas. The number of individuals affected is overwhelming, as are their stories.

Here is a short extract from the *Epilogue* of *Empty Cradles:*

'Some people have argued that allegations of physical and sexual abuse should be separated from the debate over child migration because not all of the children were affected.

I don't agree.

To take children from their families and their countries was an abuse; to strip them of their identity was an abuse; to forget them and then deny their loss was an abuse. Within this context and within our culture, few tragedies can compare.'

As I write this there are moves afoot to help some of the individuals affected claim compensation for the travesties they had to endure and I wish them well with that. In 2010 the British government finally issued an apology to the child migrants and just recently, in 2018, the Australian prime minister has given a national apology to the victims of child sexual abuse.

But there is much more that needs to be done. *Empty Cradles* is a book that everyone should read; maybe only then will we be wise enough never to let this happen again.

Thank you

As part of my research for this book I have travelled many miles and in doing so, I have tried to imagine what it must have been like for people like Patrick and Thomas. I spent a fascinating afternoon at the Immigration Museum in Melbourne, as well as a peaceful week on the Isle of Anglesey. I found a cottage that formed the inspiration for *Martha's Cottage*, just close to a bench that made me think of Walter.

I read many accounts from child migrants and am grateful for their honesty and bravery in speaking out.

I consider myself very fortunate to have the encouragement and support of some wonderful people. This book has been a long time in development and yet my brilliant writing buddies, Chris and Sarah have been beside me all the way, with invaluable critiques, as well as inspiration to keep going.

Julia helped me with some excellent editing advice, advising on last-minute adjustments that I hope have enhanced the final version.

While I am grateful to all the people who contributed to my research and writing, the mistakes and inaccuracies are all my own.

Heartfelt thanks also go to family and friends too numerous to list here. I am grateful to you all.

And, of course, my wonderful husband, Al, who continues to believe in me whatever I choose to do. Last, but never least, is our gorgeous Scottie dog, Hamish, who was there by my feet during the early mornings and late nights - keeping my feet warm.

About the author

Isabella has been surrounded by books her whole life and – after working for twenty years as a technical editor and having successfully completed her MA in Professional Writing - she was inspired to focus on fiction writing.

She is the author of the much-loved series of Sussex Crime Mystery novels, featuring young librarian and amateur sleuth, Janie Juke. The novels are set in the fictional seaside town of Tamarisk Bay, during the late sixties and seventies.

Isabella grew up in East Sussex and spent most of her life there. So when she writes about Hastings and Brighton, she writes with first-hand knowledge of all the nooks and crannies in these towns.

Now she lives in West Sussex; because aside from books, Isabella has a love of all things caravan-like. She has spent many winters caravanning in Europe and now, together with her husband, she runs a small caravan site in West Sussex. They are ably assisted by their much-loved Scottie, Hamish.

To find out more about Isabella Muir and her forthcoming titles, visit: **www.isabellamuir.com** or follow her on Twitter @SussexMysteries

By the same author

THE SUSSEX CRIME MYSTERY SERIES
Book 1: The Tapestry Bag
Book 2: Lost Property
Book 3: The Invisible Case

THE SUSSEX CRIME MYSTERIES:
A Janie Juke trilogy

Ivory Vellum: an anthology of short stories

If you enjoyed this book, then you can help other readers to discover it too, by leaving a review on any of the online book review websites.

Thank you

Lightning Source UK Ltd.
Milton Keynes UK
UKHW012226161118
332477UK00001B/160/P